Classics

JOHN COOPER

ANDERSEN'S FAIRY TALES

This book belongs
to : Dora

ANDERSEN'S
FAIRY TALES

Published by Peter Haddock Ltd.
Bridlington, England. ©

Printed in Russia.

CONTENTS

ANDERSEN'S FAIRY TALES

THE FIR-TREE

Far away in the deep forest there once grew a pretty little Fir-Tree. The sun shone full upon him; the breezes played freely round him; and near him grew many other fir-trees, some older, some younger; but the little Fir-Tree was not happy, for he always longed to be tall like the others. He thought not of the warm sun and the fresh air; he cared not for the merry, prattling peasant children who came to the forest to look for strawberries and raspberries. Sometimes, after having filled their pitches, or threaded the bright berries on a straw, they would sit down near the little Fir-Tree and say, 'What a pretty little tree this is!' and then the Fir-Tree would feel more unhappy than ever.

'Oh that I were as tall as the other trees,' sighed the little Fir, 'then I should spread my branches on every side, and my top should look out over the wide world! The birds would build their nests among my branches, and when the wind blew I should bend my head so grandly, just as the others do!' He had no pleasure in the sunshine, in the song of the birds, or in the rosy clouds that sailed over him every morning and evening.

In winter, when the ground was covered with the white glistening snow; a hare would sometimes come scampering along, and jump right over the little Tree's head; and then how miserable he felt! However, two winters passed away, and by the third the Tree was so tall that the hare was obliged to run round it. 'Oh, if I could but grow and grow, and become tall and old!' thought the Tree. 'That is the only thing in the world worth living for.'

The wood-cutters came in the autumn and felled some of the largest of the trees. This happened every year, and our young Fir, who was by this time a good height, shuddered when he saw those grand trees fall with a crash to the earth. Their branches were then cut of; the stems looked so terribly naked and lanky that they could hardly be recognized. They were laid one upon another in wagons, and horses drew them away, far, far away from the forest.

Where could they be going? What would happen to them? The Fir-Tree wished very much to know, so in the spring, when the swallows and the storks returned, he asked them if they knew where the felled trees had been taken.

The swallows knew nothing; but the stork looked thoughtful for a moment, then nodded his head and said, 'Yes, I believe I have seen them! As I was flying from Egypt I met many ships; and they had fine new masts that smelt like fir. I have little doubt that they were the trees that you speak of. They were stately, very stately, I assure you!'

'Oh that I too were tall enough to sail upon the sea! Tell me what is this sea, and what does it look like!'

'That,' said the stork, 'would take too long!' and away he stalked.

'Rejoice in your youth!' said the sunbeams; 'rejoice in your fresh youth, in the young life that is within you!'

And the wind kissed the Tree, and the dew wept tears over him, but the Fir-Tree did not understand them.

When Christmas drew near, many quite young trees were felled, some of them not so tall as the young Fir-Tree who was always longing to be away. These young trees were chosen for their beauty. Their branches were not cut off. They too were laid in a waggon, and horses drew them away from the forest.

'Where are they going?' asked the Fir-Tree. 'They are no taller than I; indeed, one of them is much less.

Why do they keep all their branches? Where can they be going?'

'We know! We know!' twittered the sparrows. 'We peeped through the windows in the town below! We know where they are gone. Oh, you cannot think what honour is done to them! We looked through the windows and saw them planted in a warm room, and decked out with such beautiful things: gilded apples, sweetmeats, playthings, and hundreds of bright candles!'

'And then?' asked the Fir-Tree, trembling in every branch; 'and then? What happened then?'

'Oh, we saw no more. That was beautiful, beautiful beyond compare!'

'Is such a glorious lot to be mine?' cried the delighted Fir-Tree. 'This is far better than sailing over the sea. How I long for the time. Oh that Christmas were come! I am now tall and have many branches, like those trees that were carried away last year. Oh that I were even now in the waggon! that I were in the warm room, honoured and adorned! and then—yes, then, something still better will happen, else why should they take the trouble to decorate me? It must be that something still greater, still more splendid, must happen—but what? Oh I suffer, I suffer with longing! I know not what it is that I feel.'

'Rejoice in our love!' said the air and the sunshine. 'Rejoice in your youth and your freedom!'

But rejoice he would not. He grew taller every day. In winter and in summer he stood there clothed in green, dark green foliage. The people that saw him said, 'That is a beautiful tree!' And next Christmas he was the first that was felled. The axe cut through the wood and pith, and the Tree fell to the earth with a deep groan. The pain was so sharp he felt faint. He quite forgot to think of his good fortune, he felt so sorry at having to leave his home in the forest. He knew that he would never see again those dear old comrades, or the little bushes and flowers that had flourished under his shadow, perhaps not even the birds. Neither did he find the journey by any means pleasant.

The Tree first came to himself when, in the courtyard to which he had been taken with the other trees, he heard a man say, 'This is a splendid one, the very thing we want!'

Then came two smartly-dressed servants, and carried the Fir-Tree into a large and handsome drawing-room. Pictures hung on the walls, and on the mantelpiece stood large Chinese vases with lions on the lids. There were rocking-chairs, silken sofas, tables covered with picture-books, and toys. The Fir-Tree was placed in a large tub filled with sand; but no one could know that it was a tub, for it was hung with green cloth and stood on a rich, gaily-coloured carpet. Oh, how the Tree trembled! What was to happen next? Some young ladies, helped by servants, began to adorn him. On some branches they hung little nets cut out of coloured paper, every net filled with sugar plums; from others gilded apples and walnuts were hung, looking just as if they had grown there; and hundreds of little wax tapers, red, blue, and white, were placed here and there among the branches. Dolls that looked almost like men and women—the Tree had never seen such things before—seemed dancing to and fro among the leaves, and high up, on the top of the tree, was fastened a large star of gold tinsel. This was indeed, splendid, splendid beyond compare.

'This evening,' they said, 'this evening it will be lighted up.'

'Would that it were evening,' thought the Tree. 'Would that the lights were kindled, for then,—what will happen then? Will the trees come out of the forest to see me? Will the sparrows fly here and look in through the window-panes? Shall I stand here adorned both winter and summer?'

He thought much of it. He thought till he had barkache with longing, and barkaches with trees are as bad as head-aches with us.

The candles were lighted—oh, what a blaze of splendour! The Tree trembled in all his branches so that a candle caught one of the twigs and set it on fire. 'Oh dear! cried the young ladies, and put it out at once.

So the Tree dared not tremble again: he was so fearful of losing any of his beautiful ornaments. He felt bewildered by all this glory and brightness. And now, all of a sudden, both folding-doors were flung open, and a troop of children rushed in as if they had a mind to jump over him; the older people followed more quietly. The little ones stood quite silent, but only for a moment. Then they shouted with delight. They shouted till the room rang again; they danced round the Tree, and one present after another was torn down.

'What are they doing?' thought the Tree. 'What will happen now?' The candles burnt down to the branches, and as each burnt down it was put out. The children were given leave to strip the Tree. They drew themselves on him till all his branches creaked; and had he not been fastened with the gold star to the ceiling he would have been overturned.

The children danced about with their beautiful playthings. No one thought of the Tree any more except the old nurse. She came and peeped among the branches, but it was only to see if, perchance, a fig or an apple had been left among them.

'A story! a story!' cried the children, pulling a little, fat man towards the Tree. 'It is pleasant to sit under the shade of green boughs,' said he, sitting down; 'besides, the tree may be benefited by hearing my story. But I shall only tell one tale. Would you like to hear about Ivedy Avedy? or about Humpty Dumpty, who fell downstairs, and yet came to the throne and won the Princess?'

'Ivedy Avedy!' cried some; 'Humpty Dumpty!' cried others. There was a great uproar. The Fir-Tree alone was silent, thinking to himself, 'Ought I to make a noise as they do? or ought I to do nothing at all?' For he most certainly was one of the company, and had done all that had been required of him.

And the little fat, man told the story of Humpty Dumpty

who fell downstairs, and yet came to the throne and won
the Princess. And the children clapped their hands and
called out for another; they wanted to hear the story of
Ivedy Avedy also, but they did not get it. The Fir-Tree
stood meanwhile quite silent and thoughtful; the birds in
the forest had never related anything like this. 'Humpty
Dumpty fell downstairs, and yet was raised to the throne
and won the Princess! Yes, yes, strange things come to
pass in the world!' thought the Fir-Tree, who believed
it must all be true, because such a pleasant man had told it.
'Who knows but I, too, may fall downstairs and win a
princess?' And he thought with delight of being next day
again decked out with candles and playthings, gold and
fruit. 'Tomorrow I will not trouble,' thought he. 'I
will thoroughly enjoy my splendour. Tomorrow I shall
hear again the story of Humpty Dumpty, and perhaps also
that about Ivedy Avedy.' And the Tree mused upon this
all night.

In the morning the maids came in. 'Now begins my
state anew!' thought the Tree. But they dragged him out
of the room, up the stairs, and into a garret, and there
thrust him into a dark corner where not a ray of light could
enter. 'What can be the meaning of this?' thought the
Tree. 'What am I to do here? What shall I hear in this
place?' And he leant against the wall, and thought, and
thought. And he had plenty of time for thinking it over;
for day after day and night after night passed away, and
yet no one ever came into the room. At last somebody did
come in, but it was only to push some old trunks into the
corner. The Tree was now entirely hidden from sight and
apparently quite forgotten.

'It is now winter,' thought the Tree. 'The ground is
hard and covered with snow; they cannot plant me now,
so I am to stay here in shelter till the spring. Men are
so thoughtful! I only wish it were not so dark and so
lonely!'

'Squeak! squeak!' cried a little mouse, just then
gliding forward. Another followed; they snuffed about

the Fir-Tree, and then slipped in and out among the branches.

'It is horribly cold!' said a little mouse; 'or it would be quite comfortable here. Don't you think so, you old Fir-Tree?'

'I am not old,' said the Fir-Tree; 'there are many who are much older than I.'

'How came you here?' asked the mice, 'and what do you know?' They were most uncommonly inquisitive. 'Tell us about the most delightful place on earth! Have you ever been there? Have you been into the store-room, where cheeses lie on the shelves, and hams hang from the ceiling; where one can dance over tallow candles; where one goes in thin and comes out fat?'

'I know nothing about that,' said the Tree, 'but I know the forest, where the sun shines and where the birds sing!' And then he spoke of his youth and its pleasures. The little mice had never heard anything like it before. They listened very closely and said, 'Well, to be sure! How much you have seen! How happy you have been!'

'Happy!' said the Fir-Tree, in surprise, and he thought a moment over all that he had been saying,—'yes, on the whole those were pleasant times!' He then told them about the Christmas Eve when he had been dressed up with cakes and candles.

'Oh!' cried the little mice, 'how happy you have been, you old Fir-Tree!'

'I am not old at all!' returned the Fir. 'It was only this winter that I left the forest; I am just in the prime of life!'

'How well you can talk!' said the little mice, and the next night they came again and brought with them four other little mice, who wanted also to hear the Tree's history. And the more the Tree spoke of his youth in the forest, the more clearly he remembered it: 'Yes,' said he, 'those were pleasant times! but they may come back, they may come back! Humpty Dumpty fell downstairs, and yet for all that he won the Princess; perhaps I, too, may win a princess!' And then the Fir thought of a pretty little delicate birch that grew in the forest, a real, and, to the Fir-Tree, a very lovely princess.

'Who's Humpty Dumpty?' asked the mice. In answer, the Fir told the tale. He could remember every word of it perfectly; and the little mice were ready to jump with joy. Next night more mice came; and on Sunday there came also two rats. The rats, however, did not find the story was at all amusing, and this annoyed the little mice, who, after hearing their opinion, could not like it so well either.

'Do you know only that one story?' asked the rats.

'Only that one!' answered the Tree. 'I heard it on the happiest evening of my life, though I did not then know how happy I was.'

'It is a miserable story! Do you know none about pork and tallow? No store-room story?'

'No,' said the Tree.

'Well, then, we have heard enough of it!' returned the rats, and they went away.

The mice, too, never came again. The Tree sighed, 'It was pleasant when those busy little mice sat round me, listening to my words. Now that, too, is past! However, I shall have pleasure in remembering it, when I am taken from this place.'

But when would that be? One morning people came, and routed out the lumber-room. The trunks were taken away: the Tree, too, was dragged out of the corner. They threw him on the floor, but one of the servants picked him up and carried him downstairs. Once more he beheld the light of day. 'Now life begins again!' thought the Tree. He felt the fresh air, the warm sunbeams—he was out in the court. All happened so quickly that the Tree quite forgot to look at himself,—there was so much to look at all around. The court joined a garden. Everything was so fresh and blooming: roses so bright and so fragrant clustered round the trellis-work, the lime-trees were in full blossom, and the swallows flew backwards and forwards, twittering.

'I shall live! I shall live!' He was filled with delight

and hope. He tried to spread out his branches; but alas!
they were all dried up and yellow. He was thrown down
on a heap of weeds and nettles. The star of gold tinsel
that had been left on his crown now sparkled in the sunshine. Some children were playing in the court, the same
merry youngsters who at Christmas-time had danced round
the Tree. One of the youngest of them saw the gold star,
and ran to tear it off.

'Look at this, still fastened to the ugly old Christmas
Tree!' cried he, trampling upon the boughs till they broke
under his boots.

And the Tree looked on the flowers of the garden now
blooming in the freshness of their beauty; he looked upon
himself, and he wished from his heart that he had been left
to wither alone in the dark corner of the lumber-room. He
called to mind his happy forest life, the merry Christmas
Eve, and the little mice who had listened so eagerly when
he related the story of Humpty Dumpty.

'Past, all past!' said the poor Tree. 'Had I but been
happy, as I might have been! Past, all past!'

And the servant came and cut the Tree into small pieces;
heaped them up, and set fire to them. And the Tree groaned
deeply, and every groan sounded like a little explosion.
The children all ran up to the place and jumped about in
front of the blaze. But at each of those heavy groans the
Fir-Tree thought of a bright summer's day, of Christmas
Eve, or of Humpty Dumpty, the only story that he knew
and could tell. And at last the Tree was burned.

The boys played about in the court. On the bosom of
the youngest sparkled the gold star that the Tree had worn
on the happiest evening of his life; but that was past, and
the Tree was past and the story also, past! past! for all
stories must come to an end some time or other.

THE SWINEHERD

There was once a poor Prince, who had a kingdom. His kingdom was small, but was still large enough to marry upon; and he wished to marry.

His name was known far and wide; and there were a hundred princesses who would each have answered 'Yes!' and 'Thank you kindly!' if he had asked her to be his wife; but he wished to marry the Emperor's daughter.

It happened that on the grave of the Prince's father there grew a rose-tree—a most beautiful rose-tree. It blossomed only once in every five years, and even then it bore only one rose—but what a rose! It was so sweet that whoever breathed its scent forgot all cares and sorrows.

And further, the Prince had a nightingale, who could sing as though all sweet melodies dwelt in her little throat. So he put the rose and the nightingale into silver caskets, and sent them to the Princess.

The Emperor had them brought into a large hall, where the Princess was playing at 'Visiting' with her maids of honour; and when she saw the caskets with the presents, she clapped her hands for joy.

'Oh, I do hope it is a little pussy-cat!' said she—but the rose-tree with its beautiful flower was brought out.

'Oh, how prettily it is made!' said all the court ladies.

'It is more than pretty,' said the Emperor; 'it is charming!'

But the Princess touched it, and was almost ready to cry.

'Pah! papa,' said she, 'it is not made at all; it is natural!'

And all the court ladies said, 'Pah! it's a natural rose.'

'Let us see what is in the other casket, before we get into a bad humour,' said the Emperor. So the nightingale came forth, and sang so delightfully that at first no one could say anything ill-humoured of her.

Superbe! charmant!' cried the ladies; for they all used to chatter French, each one worse than her neighbour.

'How the bird reminds me of the musical-box that belonged to our blessed Empress! said an old knight. 'Oh yes! these are the same tones, the same phrasing.'

'Yes! yes!' said the Emperor, and he wept at the remembrance.

'I do hope that it is not a real bird,' said the Princess.

'Yes, it is a real bird,' said those who had brought it.

'Well, then, let it fly,' said the Princess; and she refused to see the Prince.

However, he was not to be discouraged. He daubed his face over brown and black, pulled his cap over his eyes, and knocked at the door.

'Good-day to my lord the Emperor!' said he. 'Can I be taken into your service at the palace?'

'Why, yes,' said the Emperor. 'I want some one to take care of the pigs, for we have a great many of them.'

So the Prince was made 'Imperial Swineherd'. He had a dirty little room close by the pig-sties; and there he sat the whole day, and worked. By the evening he had made a pretty little kitchen-pot with bells all round it. When the pot boiled, these bells tinkled in the most charming way, and played the old tune:

> Ah! my dearest Augustine,
> All is gone, gone, gone!

But what was still more curious, whoever held his finger in the steam of the kitchen-pot immediately smelt all the dishes that were cooking on every hearth in the city.

Now the Princess happened to walk that way; and when she heard the tune, she stood quite still, and seemed greatly pleased; for it was the only piece she knew, and she played it with one finger.

'Why, there is my piece!' said the Princess. 'That swineherd must have been well educated! Go in and ask him the price of the instrument.'

So one of the ladies ran in; but she drew on wooden slippers first.

'What will you take for the kitchen-pot?' said the lady.

'Ten kisses from the Princess,' said the swineherd.

'He is an impudent fellow!' said the Princess when she heard this, and she walked on. But when she had gone a little way, the bells tinkled so prettily that she had to stop.

'Stay,' said the Princess. 'Ask him if he will have ten kisses from the ladies of my court.'

'No, thank you!' said the swineherd; 'ten kisses from the Princess, or I keep the kitchen-pot myself.'

'That must not be either!' said the Princess; 'but do you all stand before me that no one may see us.'

So the court ladies placed themselves in front of her, and spread out their dresses; the swineherd got ten kisses and the Princess—the kitchen-pot.

That was delightful! the pot was boiling the whole evening, and the whole of the following day. They knew perfectly well what was cooking at every fire throughout the city, from the chamberlain's to the cobbler's. The court ladies danced, and clapped their hands.

The swineherd let not a day pass without making something. One day he made a rattle which, when it was swung round, played all the waltzes and jig tunes that have ever been heard.

'Ah, that is *superbe*!' said the Princess when she passed by. 'I have never heard prettier compositions! Go in and ask him the price of the instrument; but mind, he shall have no more kisses!'

'He will have a hundred kisses from the Princess!' said the lady who had been to ask.

'I think he is out of his senses!' said the Princess, and walked on; but when she had gone a little way, she stopped again. 'One must encourage the fine arts,' said she. 'I am the Emperor's daughter. Tell him, he shall, as yesterday, have ten kisses from me, and may take the rest from the ladies of the court.'

'Oh!—but we should not like that at all!' said they.

'What are you muttering?' asked the Princess. 'If I can kiss him, surely you can!' So the ladies were obliged to go to him again.

'One hundred kisses from the Princess!' said he, 'or I keep the rattle.'

'Stand round us then!' said the Princess; and all the ladies stood round them whilst the kissing was going on.

'What can be the reason for such a crowd close by the pig-sties?' said the Emperor, who happened just then to step out on the balcony. He rubbed his eyes and put on his spectacles. 'They are the ladies of the court; I must go down and see what they are about!'

The ladies were so much taken up with counting the kisses that they did not notice the Emperor. He rose on his tiptoes.

'What is all this?' said he, when he saw what was going on; and he boxed the Princess's ears, just as the swineherd was taking the eighty-sixth kiss.

'Begone!' said the Emperor, for he was very angry; and both Princess and swineherd were thrust out of the city.

The Princess wept, the swineherd scolded, and the rain poured down.

'Alas! unhappy creature that I am!' said the Princess. 'If I had but married the handsome young Prince! Ah, how unfortunate I am!'

The swineherd went behind a tree, washed the dirt from his face, threw off his old clothes, and stepped forth in all his princely robes; he looked so noble that the Princess could not help bowing before him.

'I have come to despise you,' said he. 'You would not have an honourable Prince! You could not prize the rose and the nightingale, but you were ready to kiss the swineherd for the sake of a trumpery plaything. You are rightly served.'

He then went back to his own little kingdom, and shut the door of his palace in her face. Now she might well sing:

> Ah! my dearest Augustine,
> All is gone, gone, gone!

THE ROSE-ELF

In the middle of a garden grew a rose-tree covered with lovely roses, and in one of these, the loveliest of all, dwelt a little elf. He was so very little that no human eye could see him. He had a sleeping-room behind each rose-leaf. He was fair and slender as only a child can be, and had wings that reached from his shoulders to his feet. Oh! what a sweet odour there was in his chambers, and how clean and beautiful the walls were! They were the pale pink rose-leaves.

He spent the whole day basking in the warm sunshine, flying from flower to flower, dancing on the wings of flying butterflies, and reckoning how many steps it took him to run over all the roads and footpaths of a single lime-leaf; for what we call the veins of the leaf were to him roads and footpaths, and he found them almost endless. The sun set before he had ended his journey. He had set off too late.

It grew very cold; the dew fell fast, the wind blew, the best thing he could do was to hurry home. But though he made all the haste he could the roses were all closed; and he could not get in—not a single rose was open. The poor little elf was greatly frightened. He had never before been out in the night air, but had always slept sweetly and softly behind the warm rose-leaves. Certainly, this night would be the death of him!

At the other end of the garden he knew that there was an arbour of honeysuckles, whose flowers looked like great painted horns. So he made up his mind to get into one of these, and sleep there till morning. Accordingly, he flew to the spot. But hush!—there were two persons in the arbour—a handsome young man and a beautiful girl. They sat close together, wishing that they might never need to part again: they loved each other so much, more than the best child can love his father and mother.

'And yet we must part!' said the young man. 'Your brother hates us, and that is why he sends me far away on business over the mountains, and across the ocean. Farewell, my sweet bride, for surely you are my bride!'

Then they kissed each other, and the young girl wept, and gave him a rose; but before giving it to him she pressed on it a kiss so warm that the flower opened, and the little elf flew in and leant his head against the delicate, fragrant walls. He could hear distinctly the words, 'Farewell, farewell!' and he felt that the rose was placed in the young man's bosom. Oh, how the heart was throbbing! The little elf could not sleep at all for hearing the beats. The rose was not suffered to remain long in its warm resting-place. The man soon took it out, and whilst walking alone through the dark wood he kissed the flower so often and so vehemently that our tiny elf was well-nigh squeezed to death. He could feel through the rose-leaves how the man's lips were burning, and the rose opened more and more, just as though the hot midday sun were shining upon it.

But there came another man through the wood, looking gloomy and wrathful. It was the beautiful girl's wicked brother. He drew out a sharp knife, and, while the lover was kissing the rose, stabbed him to the heart, cut off his head, and buried both head and body in the moist earth under a lime-tree.

'Now we are rid of him!' thought the wicked brother; 'and he will never come back again. He was to have taken a long journey over the mountains and beyond the sea; men often lose their lives in travelling as he has done! He will never come back again, and my sister dare not question me about him.'

So he scraped with his foot some withered leaves over the upturned earth, and then walked home through the darkness. But he did not go alone, as he thought; the tiny elf went with him, rolled up in a withered lime-leaf which had fallen into the wicked man's hair while he was digging the grave. The man put on his hat, and then it was dark for our little elf, who was underneath; trembling with horror and indignation at the shameful deed he had witnessed.

In the early morning the wicked man reached his home. He took off his hat, and went into his sister's sleeping-room. The bright and beautiful girl lay there dreaming of him whom she loved so well, and who, she supposed, was now wandering far away across mountain and forest. Her wicked brother bent over her, and laughed a hateful laugh, a laugh like that of a fiend. The withered leaf fell out of his hair upon the counterpane, but he did not notice it, and went away intending to sleep a little himself in the early morning hours. The elf now glided out of the withered leaf, crept to the ear of the sleeping girl, and told her, as though in a dream, all about the horrible murder. He described to her the spot where her brother had slain her lover, and had buried the body, close under the lime-trees in full blossom, and added: 'In token that all I have told you is not a mere dream, you shall find a withered leaf upon your bed when you awake.'

Oh, what bitter tears she shed when she awoke and found the withered lime-leaf on her bed! But she dared not speak to any one of her great sorrow. The window was left open all day, so that the little elf could easily have flown out to the roses and other flowers in the garden; but he could not find it in his heart to leave one who was so unhappy. A monthly rose-tree stood at the window; he got into one of its flowers, and sat looking at the poor girl. Her brother often came into the room, and seemed very merry, but she dared not speak a word to him of her heart's sorrow.

As soon as it was night she stole out of the house, and going to the wood, to the place where the lime-tree grew, she swept away the dry leaves, and dug in the earth till she found the corpse of the murdered man. Oh, how she wept and prayed to God that she too might die soon!

Gladly would she have taken the body home with her

but that she could not do. So she took up the head, kissed the pale, cold lips and closed eyes, and shook the earth out of the beautiful hair. 'This I will keep!' said she, and covering the dead body afresh with earth, she returned home, taking with her the head and a little bough from a jasmine-tree that blossomed near the grave. When she reached home she fetched the largest flower-pot she could find, put into it the head of the dead man, covered it over with mould, and planted the slip of jasmine above it.

'Farewell, farewell!' whispered the little elf. He could no longer bear to witness so much misery, and he flew into the garden to his own rose. But he found it faded, and only a few pale leaves still clinging to the green hedge behind. 'Alas! how quickly does everything good and beautiful pass away!' sighed the elf. At last he found another rose that would suit for his home, and laid himself down among its fragrant leaves. And he flew every morning to the window of the poor girl's room, and every morning he found her standing over the flower-pot weeping. Her salt tears fell upon the jasmine, and day by day, as she grew paler and paler, the plant grew fresher and greener. One little shoot after another pushed forth, and the delicate white buds unfolded into flowers. And she kissed the flowers, but her wicked brother mocked her, and asked her if she had lost her wits. He could not bear it, and he could not understand why she was always weeping over that jasmine. He did not know whose closed eyes were resting there, nor whose red lips were fading beneath the earth.

One day she leaned her head against the flower-pot, and the little rose-elf flew into the room and found her sleeping. He crept into her ear, and talked to her of what he had heard in the arbour on that sad evening, of the fragrance of the roses, and of the love that the flower-spirits bore her. She dreamed very sweetly, and while she was dreaming her life slipped away calmly and gently, and her spirit, now at perfect peace, was in heaven with him whom she had loved so dearly.

And the blossoms of the jasmine opened their large white bells, and sent forth a fragrance wonderfully sweet and strong; this was the only way in which they could bewail the dead.

But the wicked brother saw the beautiful, blooming tree, and considering it now his own, he took it away into his sleeping-room and placed it near the bed, for it was very beautiful and its fragrance was delightful. The little rose-elf followed it, flew from flower to flower, for in each flower there dwelt a little spirit, and to each he told of the murdered young man whose head was now dust with the dust under their roots, of the wicked brother and the heart-broken sister.

'We know it!' replied all the spirits of the flowers; 'we know it! Have not we sprung from the eyes and lips of the murdered man? We know it, we know it!' And they all nodded their heads in the strangest manner.

The rose-elf could not understand how they could take it so quietly, and he flew away to the bees, who were gathering honey in the garden, and told the story to them. And the bees told their Queen, and she gave orders that next morning they should all go and kill the murderer.

That very same night, however—it was the first night after his sister's death—whilst the brother was asleep in the bed near which the jasmine-tree was placed, each little flower-cup opened, and out flew the flower-spirits, invisible, but armed each with a poisoned arrow. They first crept into his ear and made him dream of his sinful deed, and then flew through his parted lips, and stabbed him in the tongue with their poisonous shafts.

'Now we have avenged the dead!' said they, and they flew back into the white jasmine-cups.

After day had dawned, the bedroom window being suddenly flung open, the rose-elf flew in, followed by the Queen-bee and her whole swarm; they had come to sting the murderer to death. But he was already dead; some persons were standing round the bed, declaring, 'The strong scent of the jasmines has killed him!'

*The rose-elf flew in followed by the Queen-bee and
her whole swarm*

The rose-elf then understood that the flower-spirits had taken vengeance on the murderer. He explained it to the Queen-bee, and she, with her whole swarm, buzzed round the flower-pot in token of approval. In vain did people try to drive them off. At last a man took up the flower-pot, intending to carry it away, whereupon one of the bees stung him in the hand, so that the pot fell to the ground and broke in pieces.

All who were present then saw the beautiful curling hair of the murdered youth, and guessed that the dead man in the bed must be a murderer.

And the Queen-bee flew buzzing about in the garden, singing of the vengeance of the flowers, of the rose-elf, and how that behind the tiniest leaf there lurks a spirit who knows when crime is committed, and can punish the evil-doer.

THE STORY OF THE YEAR

It was far on in the month of January, and the snow was falling heavily. It whirled through the streets and lanes of the town; it plastered the window-panes; it fell in heaps from the roofs. Every one was in a hurry. The people rushed blindly on their way, ran against one another caught one another by the arms to keep themselves from falling and then sped on again. Coaches and horses looked as if they had been powdered with sifted sugar. The foot-men stood with their backs turned to the carriages, so as not to face the wind, and the foor-passengers crept along in the shelter of these vehicles as they crawled slowly through the deep snow.

When the storm abated, a narrow pathway was swept clean in front of the houses, and when two people met on this they stood stock-still, neither being willing to step into the deep snow at the side to let the other pass. After a moment's motionless silence, as if by mutual agreement each sacrificed one leg, burying it in the snow-heap, and so passed on his way.

Towards evening the weather became better. The sky grew clear, and looked as if, where the snow had been swept away, it had become loftier and more transparent. The stars shone with fresh brightness and purity. It froze so hard that underfoot the snow crackled, and by dawn its surface had grown firm enough to support the sparrows that hopped upon it, searching for food on the pathway that had been swept. Poor, shivering little things! they found that there was hardly anything for them.

'Tweet! tweet!' said one to another. 'They call this a new year! We might just as well have been content with the old, for this seems to me worse. I don't know how you feel, but I can assure you I am utterly miserable.'

'You're quite right,' said a shivering little sparrow, 'and yet people fired off guns and made a great fuss to welcome in the New Year. They clapped their hands, threw their caps in the air, and seemed quite mad; they were so glad the old year was gone. I was glad too, for I hoped for warm weather; but it freezes harder, I think, than it did before. Surely people must have made a mistake in the time.'

'That they have,' said a white-headed old sparrow. 'Men have a thing they call a Calendar, a contrivance of their own, and everything must be arranged according to it. But in some ways it's really too absurd; the year begins when Spring comes. Nature says so, and I trust Nature.'

'But when will Spring come?' inquired the others.

'Spring will come when the stork returns,' answered the old sparrow; 'but then the movements of the stork are never quite certain, and here in town no one knows anything about them. In the country people know better. Shall we fly off to the country and wait there? At least we shall then be nearer the Spring.'

'That's all very well,' said another little bird, who for some time had been hopping about and chirping, but without saying anything worth repeating; 'but I have found some comforts here in the town that I am afraid I should not find in the country. A family lives near this who have had the good sense to place three or four flower-pots against the wall of the courtyard, with their mouths to the wall and their bottoms pointing outwards. In these holes have been cut large enough for me to fly in and out; so in one pot my husband and I have built our nest, and there all our young ones, who have now flown away, were reared. Of course the family put the pots there that they might have the pleasure of seeing us; they could have had no other reason for doing so. It has pleased them, too, to scatter bread-crumbs for us, so that we have both food and shelter, and may consider ourselves very well off. So I think that my husband and I will stay where we are. There are some drawbacks, but all the same we will stay.'

'Let us fly away into the country,' cried the others, 'to see if the Spring is coming.' So away they flew. In the country the weather was more severe and the cold some degrees stronger than in the town. Biting blasts blew across the snow-covered fields. The farmer, heavily clad and with thick woollen gloves on his hands, sat in his cart, the whip on his knees, and beat his arms across his breast to warm himself. The farm horses ran till they steamed. The crisp snow crackled beneath their feet, and the sparrows hopped in the wheel-ruts and shivered, crying 'Tweet! tweet! when will the Spring come? It is very long in coming.'

'Very long indeed,' came far across the field the cry from the nearest snow-covered hill. It might have been an echo that they heard, or perhaps it was the cry of the wonderful old man who, regardless of wind and weather, sat there, high on a heap of snow. He was all in white, dressed, peasant-like, in a coat of coarse frieze. His face was pale, and he had long white hair and big blue eyes.

'Who is that old man?' asked the sparrows.

'I can tell you,' said an old raven who was seated on the fence, and being wise enough to understand that in the sight of heaven we are all alike little birds, was not above speaking to common sparrows and giving them the informa-tion they asked. 'I know who the old man is. It is the Winter, the old man of last year. He is not dead, though the calendar says he is; but is guardian for the little Prince Spring, who is coming. Yes, Winter still rules here. O-o! how the cold makes one shiver, my dears!'

'Isn't that what I told you?' said the smallest of the sparrows. 'The Calendar is just a contrivance of man, and is not at all a natural one. On such subjects men should really consult us, who are by nature so much cleverer than they.'

First one week passed, and then a second. The hard-frozen lake looked like a sheet of lead. A cold damp fog hung over the land. Silently, and in long rows, the great black crows flew about. It seemed as if all things were asleep. Then a sunbeam glided over the lake, causing it to shine like polished silver; but the snow on field and fell did not glitter so brightly as before. Still the white form of Winter himself sat there, staring fixedly southwards. He did not see the snow carpet sinking into the ground, or the small green patches of grass coming into view here and there, or the sparrows that gathered on them in crowds.

'Twee-weet! tee-weet! Is Spring coming at last?' they twittered.

'The Spring!' Thy cry rung out o'er field and meadow, and through the dark-brown woods where the fresh green moss still brightened the tree trunks; and from the south came the first two storks flying through the air. On the back of each was a lovely little child, a boy and a girl. They greeted the earth with a kiss, and wherever their feet were set, the white flowers sprang up from beneath the snow. Hand in hand the two children went to the old ice man Winter, threw their arms round him and clung to his breast. In a moment the three, and all the region round were shrouded in a dense damp mist, that like a thick black veil closed over all. Slowly the wind rose, until with blustering noise and sturdy thrusts it pushed away the mist. Then the sun shone out warmly; Winter himself had vanished, and the lovely children of Spring sat on the throne of the year. 'That's what I call a New Year!' said each little sparrow. 'Now we shall have our dues, and get some amends for what we suffered in winter.'

Wherever the children wandered the green buds burst forth on the trees and bushes; the grass sprang up; and the cornfields grew greener, and more and more beautiful. The girl scattered flowers in her path. She held her apron in front of her. It was always full of flowers, that seemed to grow up in it, for the more flowers she strewed, the fuller her lap was. Eagerly she showered the snowy blossoms over apple-trees and peach-trees, so that even before their green leaves had come out, the trees stood forth in full beauty.

And the maiden clapped her hands and the boy clapped

his, and flocks of birds came flying up no one knew from whence; and they all twittered and sang, 'Spring has come!' How astonishingly beautiful everything was. Old dames crawled forth from their houses into the sunshine, and tripped joyously about, watching the golden blossoms that glittered everywhere in the fields, just as they used to when they were young. For them the world again grew young, and they said, 'What splendid weather! What a glorious day!'

The forest still wore its dress of dark green buds; but the fresh and fragrant thyme was already in bloom. Violets grew there in abundance; primroses and anemones came forth; and every blade of grass stood stiff and full of sap, making a lovely carpet on which one could not help sitting down. And there the children of Spring sat hand in hand, and sang and laughed, and grew and grew. A gentle shower fell upon them from the sky, but they did not notice it, for the raindrops and their tears of gladness were mingled. So the betrothed bride and bridegroom kissed each other, and in a moment all the woods were green.

Hand in hand the betrothed couple wandered forth, under the fresh canopy of leaves, through the openings in which the sunbeams gleamed in ever-changing and varying hues. What virgin purity! what refreshing balm there was in the soft young lovers! Merrily laughed the clear brooks and the stream as they slid between the green velvety rushes, or rippled over the many-coloured pebbles. All Nature cried aloud, 'There is plenty, and plenty there shall always be!' And the cuckoo sang, and the lark carolled, for now it was the beautiful Spring.

Days and weeks passed, and the heat steadily increased. The warm air waved the corn which grew more and more golden. The great green leaves of the white water-lily were spread over the glassy surface of the woodland lake, and under their shadows the fishes played. In a sheltered spot in the woods, lit up by the sunlight, stood a farm-house. The heat of the sun's beams made the roses bloom on the walls and ripened the berries that hung, black and juicy, on the heavily-laden cherry-trees. Here sat Summer's charming wife, she whom we have seen as child and as bride. She was gazing fixedly at the gathering clouds, that in dense black mountain-like masses kept rolling up higher and higher their ever-changing forms. They came up from three sides, ever growing greater and greater, and like an inverted rolling sea swopped down on the forest; where, as if by magic, all was silence. Every breeze was stilled; every bird was mute; all Nature stood gravely expectant; but in the highways and byeways travellers on foot and in vehicles were hurrying to get under shelter. Then came a gleam of light, as if the sun had burst out flaming, dazzling, all-consuming—and the darkness returned again with the rolling thunder-crash. Down came the rain in torrents. One moment it was perfectly dark; the next the light was blinding. Now the silence was so intense it could be felt; in an instant the din was deafening. On the moor the young brown reeds swung to and fro in long waves; the forest boughs were hidden in a watery mist; the darkness came and was ploughed through by the light, and the deep silence was broken by the crashing roar. The grass and the corn lay beaten down and sodden-looking, as if they could never again raise themselves. In a little the rain began to fall more gently. The sun broke forth, and the raindrops glistened on leaf and stem like pearls. The birds sang in the meadows, the fish played over the surface of the water, the gnats danced in the sunbeams, and on a rock by the rolling salt-sea waves sat Summer himself, a vigorous, strong-limbered man, with long, dripping hair. Refreshed by his cold bath, he was basking in the warm sunshine. About him all Nature refreshed rose luxuriant, strong, and beautiful; it was summer, warm, charming summer. Delightfully sweet was the smell wafted from the clover field, where the bees swarmed round the ruined tower and the bramble crawled over the hearth-stone which, washed by the rain, shone in the sunshine; while thither flew the Queen-bee with her swarm, and made ready wax and honey. Summer and his buxom dame hardly observed these things, for to them the earth stood adorned with the offerings of Nature. The evening sky gleamed like gold. No minister dome ever shone so brightly; and between the red evening and the blushing dawn the pale moon shed her light. It was summer!

Days and weeks passed. In the cornfields the reapers' bright sickles flashed; the apple-tree branches drooped under their heavy load of golden fruit. The hops smelt delightfully and hung down in heavy clusters; and under the hazel-bushes, where the nuts grew in great bunches, rested a man and a woman, Summer and his sober spouse.

'What wealth,' said she, 'has been gathered around us, all homelike and good. And yet I know not why, I have an indescribable longing for peace, for rest. Now they have already begun to plough the fields again! More and ever more the people long for gain. Lo! the storks, the birds from Egypt, that carried us through the air, are flocking together, and, at a short distance behind, are following the plough. Do you remember how as children we came to this Northern land, and brought with us the flowers, and the cheerful sunshine, and the green woods? The winds have dealt harshly with them; they are grown brown and dark like the trees of the South; but, unlike them, they bear no golden fruit.'

'Do you wish to see the golden fruit?' said Summer. 'Be glad then.' So saying he raised his arm and the forest leaves arrayed themselves in red and gold, and the woodlands grew splendid with colour. The rose-bushes glowed with their scarlet hips; the elder branches hung heavily weighed down with their dark-brown berries; the wild chestnuts dropped ripe from their dark-green shells, and in the woodland the violets bloomed for the second time.

But the Queen of the Year grew more and more silent and pale. 'It grows cold,' said she. 'The night brings the damp mists. I long for the land of my childhood.'

Then she saw the storks, one and all, fly away, and she stretched forth her hands towards them. She gazed at the nests, standing up there empty. In one grew a long-stalked corn-flower; in another a yellow mustard-seed, as though the nest had been put there just for its comfort and protection.

'Tweet! tweet!' said the sparrows as they flew up into the nest of the stork. 'Where have the masters of the nest gone? They could not stand it when it grew windy, we suppose, and so they have left the country. We wish them a pleasant journey.'

The forest leaves grew yellower and yellower, and fell one after another. The winds of autumn howled. The year was now far advanced, and on the yellow fallen leaves sat the Queen of the Year, and hazed with gentle eyes at a gleaming star, while by her stood her husband. A blast swept through the leaves, which fell in a shower, and the Queen of the Summer had vanished; but a butterfly, the last of the year, fluttered through the cold air.

The damp fogs came. An ice-wind blew, and the darkness of the longest night drew near. With snow-white locks the Ruler of the Year appeared; but he himself did not know that they were white. A thin snow-covering was spreading itself over the green fields, and he thought the whiteness of his head due to the snow that fell from the sky. The church-bells rang out their Christmas chimes, and the Ruler of the Year said, 'The bells are ringing for the birth of the Year. The new Lord of the Year will soon be born, and I, like my wife, shall go to rest, to rest in yon light-giving star!'

In the fresh green wood the while stood the Christmas-angel, and consecrated the young trees that were to adorn his festival. 'May there be mirth and joy in the rooms and under the green boughs,' said the Ruler of the Old Year. In a short time he had changed to a very old man with snow-white hair. 'My resting-time draws nigh. The Year's young couple will soon claim my crown and sceptre!'

'The watch is still thine!' said the Christmas-angel. 'Thou art on guard, and thy rest is not yet! Let the snow warmly cover the young seed. Suffer another to be wor-

shipped while thou art still Lord. Bear being forgotten
while thou still livest. The hour of thy release will come
with the Spring.'

'When does Spring come?' asked Winter.

'It will come when the storks return,' answered the
Angel.

On a drift on the snowy hills, where the Winter before
had sat and gazed, Winter was seated staring southwards.
His locks were white, his beard like snow; his body bent
and chilled and smitten with years, but strong as the winter
blasts, and hard as a rock. The ice roared, the crisp snow
crackled, the skaters skimmed hither and thither over the
smooth lakes; while crows and ravens showed up well
against the white ground. No word broke the silence;
and in the calm air Winter clenched his fists and the ice
lay fathom-thick between land and land.

Then the sparrows came again out of the town and asked,
'Who is that old man?' and the raven still sat there, and
answered their questions, and said, 'It is Winter, the Old
Man of last year. He is not dead though the Calendar says
he is; but he is the guardian of the coming Spring.'

'When will Spring come?' chirped the sparrows. 'Then
we shall have a fine time of it and be better off in every
way. The old times are no good.'

Deep in thought, Winter gazed on the dark leafless
woods, where the graceful forms and curves of each tree
and branch showed; and while he slept the icy mists sank
down from the clouds, and the old Ruler dreamt of his
youth and of his manhood; and at the break of day the
whole forest sparkled with the hoar-frost. This was Winter's
summer-dream. Soon the sun shook the hoar-frost from
the boughs.

'When will Spring come?' twittered the sparrows.

'Spring!' rang like an echo from the hills on which the
snow still lay. The sun shone warmer. The snow melted.
The birds sang, 'Spring is coming.' And, aloft, through
the air came the first stork; the second followed; a lovely
child sat on the back of each, and they settled down on

the open field and kissed the earth, and kissed the silent Old Man, and like mists from the hill-tops he vanished away. The Story of the Year was finished.

'That's all very well,' said the sparrows, 'and it is very pretty, too; but it is not according to the Calendar, and therefore it must be wrong.'

THE STORKS

On the roof of a house, the last in a little village, a stork had built his nest. There sat the mother-stork with her four young ones, who all stretched out their little black bills, which had not yet become red. Not far off, on the top of the roof, erect and proud, stood the father-stork. He had drawn up one of his legs under him, being weary of standing on two. You might have thought that he was carved out of wood, he stood so motionless.

In the street below, a whole swarm of children were playing. When they saw the storks, one of the liveliest amongst them began to sing as much as he could remember of some old rhymes about storks, and he was soon joined by the others.

> Stork, stork, fly to your nest;
> And give your tired long leg a rest.
> There is stillness sits your mate
> Watching her brood with care so great.
> The first shall hang on a gallows-tree;
> Of the second the end by fire shall be;
> The third upon a spit shall roast;
> And of shooting the fourth a marksman boast.

'Only listen to what the boys are singing,' said the little storks; 'they say we shall be hanged and burnt!'

'Never mind,' said the mother. 'Don't listen to them, and it will do you no harm.'

But the boys went on singing, and pointed their fingers at the storks. Only one little boy, called Peter, said it was a sin to mock and tease animals, and that he would have nothing to do with it.

The mother-stork again tried to comfort her little ones.

'Never mind,' said she; 'see how quietly your father is standing there, and upon one leg only.'

'But we are so frightened!' said the young ones, drawing their heads down into the nest.

The next day, when the children were again playing together, and saw the storks, they began to sing—

> The first shall hang on a gallows-tree;
> Of the second the end by fire shall be.

'And are we really to be hanged and burnt?' asked the young storks.

'No indeed!' said the mother. 'You shall learn to fly: I will teach you myself. Then we can fly over to the meadow, and pay a visit to the frogs. They will bow to us in the water, and say, 'Croak, croak!' and then we shall eat them. Will not that be nice?'

'And what then?' asked the little storks.

'Then all the storks in the country will gather together, and the autumn manœuvres will begin. It is of the greatest importance that you should fly well then; for the general will stab to death with his bill every one who does not. So you must pay great attention when we begin to drill you, and learn very quickly. After the great review is over, we shall fly far, far away from here, over mountains and forests, to a warm country where we shall have nothing to do but eat frogs all the day long. And whilst we are so well off there, in this country not a single green leaf is left on the trees, and it is so cold that the clouds are frozen, and fall down upon the earth in little white pieces.'—She meant snow, but she could not express herself more clearly.

'And will the naughty boys be frozen to pieces too?' asked the young storks.

'No, they will not be frozen to pieces; but they will be nearly as badly off as if they were. They will be obliged to crowd round the fire in their little dark rooms; while we shall be flying about in foreign lands, where there are beautiful flowers and warm sunshine.'

Time passed, and the young storks grew so tall that when they stood upright in the nest they could see the country around to a great distance.

'Now you must learn to fly!' said the mother one day; and accordingly, all the four young storks were obliged to come out on the top of the roof. Oh! how they trembled! And though they balanced themselves on their wings, they were very near falling.

'Only look at me,' said the mother. 'This is the way you must hold your heads; and you must place your feet so,—one, two! one, two! this will help you to get on.' She flew a little way, and the young ones made an awkward spring after her; but, plump! down they fell; for their bodies were still too heavy.

'I will not fly,' said one of the young ones, as he crept back into the nest. 'I do not want to go to warm countries!'

'Do you want to be frozen to death during the winter? Shall the boys come, and hang, burn, or roast you? Wait a little, I will call them!'

'Oh no!' said the little stork; and again he began to hop about on the roof like the others. By the third day they could fly pretty well. The boys again came into the street, singing their favourite song—

Stork, stork, fly to your nest!

'Shall not we fly down and peck out their eyes?' said the young ones.

'No, leave them alone!' said the mother. 'Attend to me; that is of much more importance! One, two, three, now to the right!—one, two, three, now to the left, round the chimney pot! That was very well. You managed your wings so neatly that I will permit you to come with me tomorrow to the marsh.'

'All the same we shall take revenge upon those rude boys,' said the young ones.

Of all the boys in the town, the one most bent on singing

the song was the one who had begun it, a little urchin not more than six years old. The young storks indeed fancied him a hundred years old, because he was bigger than either their father or mother; and what should they know about the ages of children or of grown-up people! All their schemes of revenge were aimed at this little boy, for he had been the first to shout at them, and had continued to do so. The young storks were very angry about it, and the older they grew the angrier they were at being teased. Their mother, to pacify them, at last promised that they should be avenged, but not until the last day of their stay in that place.

'We must first see how you behave yourselves at the great review. If then you should fly badly, and the general should thrust his beak into your breast, the boys will, at least so far, be proved in the right. Let me see how well you will behave!'

'Yes, that you shall!' said the young ones. And now they really took great pains, practised every day, and at last flew so prettily that it was a pleasure to see them.

Autumn came, and all the storks assembled to make ready to fly together to warm countries for the winter. What a practising there was! Away they went over woods and fields, towns and villages, merely to see how well they could fly, for they had a long journey before them. The young storks did so well that they were pronounced 'worthy of frogs and serpents', which was the highest character they could obtain.

'Now we will have our revenge!' said they.

'Very well!' said the mother. 'I have been thinking what will be the best. I know where the pond is in which all the little human children lie until the storks come and take them to their parents. The pretty little things sleep and dream more sweetly than they will ever dream hereafter. All parents like to have a little child, and all children like to have a little brother or sister. We will fly to the pond and fetch one for each of the boys who has not sung that naughty song and made fun of the storks.'

'But the naughty ugly boy who began the song first, what shall we do to him?' cried the young storks.

'In the pond there lies a little child who has dreamed away his life. We will take it home to the naughty boy, and he will weep because he has only a little dead brother. But as to the good boy who said it was a sin to mock and tease animals, surely you have not forgotten him? We will bring him two little ones, a brother and a sister. And as this little boy's name is Peter, you too shall for the future be called "Peter".'

And it came to pass just as the mother said; and all the storks were called 'Peter', and are still so called to this very day.

THE UGLY DUCKLING

How beautiful it was in the country! It was summer-time; the wheat was yellow, the oats were green, the hay was stacked up in the verdant meadows, and the stork strutted about on his long red legs, chattering in Egyptian, the language he had learned from his mother. The fields and meadows were skirted by thick woods, and in the midst of the woods lay a deep lake. Yes, it was indeed beautiful in the country! The sunshine fell warmly on an old country house, surrounded by deep canals, and from the walls down to the water's edge there grew large burdock-leaves, so high that children could stand upright among them without being seen. This place was as wild and lonely as the thickest part of the wood, and on that account a duck had chosen to make her nest there. She was sitting on her eggs; but the pleasure she had felt at first was now almost gone, because she had been there so long, and had so few visitors, for the other ducks preferred swimming about in the canals to climbing up the slippery banks and sitting gossiping with her.

At last the eggs began to crack, and one little head after another appeared. 'Quack, quack!' said the duck, and all got up as well as they could, and peeped about from under the green leaves.

'How large the world is!' said the little ones.

'Do you think this is the whole of the world?' said the mother. 'It stretches far away beyond the other side of the garden down to the pastor's field; but I have never been there. Are you all here?' And then she got up. 'No, I have not got you all; the largest egg is still here. How long, I wonder, will this last? I am so weary of it!' And then she sat down again.

'Well! and how are you getting on?' asked an old duck, who had come to pay her a visit.

'This one egg keeps me so long,' said the mother, 'it will not break; but you should see the others! They are the prettiest little ducklings I have seen in all my days.'

'Depend upon it,' said the old duck, 'it is a turkey's egg. I was cheated in the same way once myself, and I had such trouble with the young ones. They were so afraid of the water that I could not get them to go near it. I called and scolded, but it was all of no use. But let me see the egg. Ah yes! to be sure, that is a turkey's egg. Leave it, and teach the other little ones to swim.'

'I will sit on it a little longer,' said the duck. 'I have been sitting so long, that a day or two more will not matter much.'

'It is no business of mine,' said the old duck, and away she waddled.

The great egg burst at last. 'Peep, peep!' said the little one, and out it tumbled. But oh! how large and ugly it was! The duck looked at it. 'That is a great, strong creature,' said she, 'none of the others are at all like it. Can it be a young turkey-cock? Well, we shall soon find out. Into the water it must go, though I should have to push it in myself.'

The next day there was delightful weather, and the sun was shining warmly upon all the green leaves when mother-duck with her family went down to the canal. Splash! she went into the water. 'Quack, quack!' cried she, and one duckling after another jumped in. The water closed over their heads, but all came up again, and swam quite easily. All were there, even the ugly grey one was swimming about with the rest.

'No, it is not a turkey,' said the mother-duck; 'only see how prettily it moves its legs, how upright it holds itself. It is my own child, and it is really very pretty when one looks more closely at it. Quack, quack! now come with me, I will take you into the world; but keep close to me, or some one may tread on you; and beware of the cat.

When they came into the duck-yard, two families were

quarrelling about the head of an eel, which in the end was carried off by the cat.

'See, my children, such is the way of the world,' said the mother-duck, whetting her beak, for she too was fond of roasted eels. 'Now use your legs,' said she, 'keep together, and bow to the old duck you see yonder. She is the noblest born of them all, and is of Spanish blood, which accounts for her dignified appearance and manners. And look, she has a red rag on her leg; that is considered a special mark of distinction, and is the greatest honour a duck can have.'

The other ducks who were in the yard looked at them and said aloud, 'Only see! now we have another brood, as if there were not enough of us already. And fie! how ugly that one is; we will not endure it.' And immediately one of the ducks flew at him, and bit him on the neck.

'Leave him alone,' said the mother; 'he is doing no one any harm.'

'Yes; but he is so large and so ungainly.'

'Those are fine children that our good mother has,' said the old duck with the red rag on her leg. 'All are pretty except that one, who certainly is not at all well favoured. I wish his mother could improve him a little.'

'Certainly he is not handsome,' said the mother, 'but he is a very good child, and swims as well as the others, indeed rather better. I think in time he will grow like the others, and perhaps will look smaller.' And she stroked the duckling's neck, and smoothed his ruffled feathers. 'Besides,' added she, 'he is a drake; I think he will be very strong; so he will fight his way through.'

'The other ducks are very pretty,' said the old duck. 'Pray make yourselves at home, and if you find an eel's head you can bring it to me.'

And accordingly they made themselves at home.

But the poor duckling, who had come last out of his egg-shell, and who was so ugly, was bitten, pecked, and teased by both ducks and hens. And the turkey-cock, who had come into the world with spurs on, and therefore fancied he was an emperor, puffed himself up like a ship in full sail, and marched up to the duckling quite red with passion. The poor thing scarcely knew what to do; he was quite distressed because he was so ugly.

So passed the first day, and afterwards matters grew worse and worse. Even his brothers and sisters behaved unkindly, and were constantly saying, 'May the cat take you, you ugly thing!' while his mother said she wished he had never been born. The ducks bit him, the hens pecked him, and the girl who fed the poultry kicked him. He ran through the hedge, and the little birds in the bushes were frightened and flew away. 'That is because I am so ugly,' thought the duckling, and ran on. At last he came to a wide moor, where lived some wild ducks. There he lay the whole night, feeling very tired and sorrowful. In the morning the wild ducks flew up, and then they saw their new companion. 'Pray who are you?' asked they; and the duckling greeted them as politely as possible.

'You are really very ugly,' said the wild ducks; 'but that does not matter to us if you do not wish to marry into our family.'

Poor thing! he had never thought of marrying. He only wished to lie among the reeds, and drink the water of the moor. There he stayed for two whole days. On the third day there came two wild geese, or rather goslings, for they had not been long out of their egg-shells, which accounts for their impertinence.

'Hark-ye,' said they, 'you are so ugly that we like you very well. Will you go with us and become a bird of passage? On another moor, not far from this, are some dear, sweet, wild geese, as lovely creatures as have ever said 'hiss, hiss'. It is a chance for you to get a wife; you may be lucky, ugly as you are.'

Bang! a gun went off, and both goslings lay dead among the reeds. Bang! another gun went off, and whole flocks of wild geese flew up from the rushes. Again and again the same alarming noise was heard.

There was a great shooting party. The sportsmen lay

in ambush all around; some were even sitting in the trees, whose huge branches overshadowed the rushes. The dogs splashed about in the mud, bending the reeds and rushes in all directions. How frightened the poor little duck was! He turned away his head, thinking to hide it under his wing, and at the same moment a fierce-looking dog passed close to him, his tongue hanging out of his mouth, his eyes sparkling fearfully. His jaws were wide open. He thrust his nose close to the duckling, showing his sharp white teeth, and then splash, splash! he was gone—gone without hurting him.

'Well! let me be thankful,' sighed the duckling. 'I am so ugly that even a dog will not bite me.'

And so he lay still though the shooting continued among the reeds. The noise did not cease till late in the day, and even then the poor little thing dared not stir. He waited several hours before he looked around him, and then hastened away from the moor as fast as he could. He ran over fields and meadows, though the wind was so high that he could hardly go against it.

Towards evening he reached a wretched little hut, so wretched that it knew not on which side to fall, and therefore remained standing. He noticed that the door had lost one of its hinges, and hung so much awry that there was a space between it and the wall wide enough to let him through. So, as the storm was becoming worse and worse, he crept into the room.

In this room lived an old woman, with her tom-cat and her hen. The cat, whom she called her little son, knew how to set up his back and purr. He could even throw out sparks when his fur was stroked the wrong way. The hen had very short legs, and was therefore called 'Chickie Shortlegs'; she laid very good eggs, and the old woman loved her as her own child.

The next morning the cat began to mew and the hen to cackle when they saw the new guest.

'What is the matter;' asked the old woman, looking round. Her eyes were not good, so she took the duckling to be a fat duck who had lost her way. 'This is a capital catch,' said she. 'I shall now have duck's eggs, if it be not a drake. We must wait and see.' So the duckling was kept on trial for three weeks; but no eggs made their appearance.

Now the cat was the master of the house, and the hen was the mistress, and they used always to say, 'We and the world,' for they imagined themselves to be not only the half of the world, but also by far the better half. The duckling thought it was possible to be of different opinion, but that the hen would not allow.

'Can you lay eggs?' asked she.

'No.'

'Well, then, hold your tongue.'

And the cat said, 'Can you set up your back? can you purr?'

'No.'

'Well, then, you should have no opinion at all when sensible people are speaking.'

So the duckling sat in a corner feeling very much dispirited till the fresh air and bright sunshine came into the room through the open door, and these gave him such a strong desire to swim that he could not help telling the hen.

'What ails you?' said the hen. 'You have nothing to do, and therefore brood over these fancies; either lay eggs, or purr, then you will forget them.'

'But it is so delicious to swim,' said the duckling; 'so delicious when the waters close over your head, and you plunge to the bottom.'

'Well, that is a queer sort of pleasure,' said the hen; 'I think you must be crazy. Not to speak of myself, ask the cat—he is the wisest creature I know—whether he would like to swim, or to plunge to the bottom of the water. Ask your mistress: no one is cleverer than she. Do you think she would take pleasure in swimming, and in the waters closing over her head?'

'You do not understand me,' said the duckling.

'What! we do not understand you! So you think

yourself wiser than the cat and the old woman, not to speak of myself! Do not fancy any such thing, child, but be thankful for all the kindness that has been shown you. Are you not lodged in a warm room, and have you not the advantage of society from which you can learn something? But you are a chatterbox, and it is wearisome to listen to you. Believe me, I wish you well. I tell you unpleasant truths, but it is thus that real friendship is shown. Come, for once give yourself the trouble either to learn to purr, or to lay eggs.'

'I think I will take my chance and go out into the wide world again,' said the duckling.

'Well, go then,' said the hen.

So the duckling went away. He soon found water and swam on the surface and plunged beneath it; but all other animals passed him by, on account of his ugliness. The autumn came: the leaves turned yellow and brown; the wind caught them and danced them about; the air was very cold; the clouds were heavy with hail or snow, and the raven sat on the hedge and croaked. The poor duckling was certainly not very comfortable!

One evening, just as the sun was setting, a flock of large birds rose from the brushwood. The duckling had never seen anything so beautiful before; their plumage as of a dazzling white, and they had long slender necks. They were swans. They uttered a singular cry, spread out their long, splendid wings, and flew away from these cold regions to warmer countries, across the sea. They flew so high, so very high! and the ugly duckling's feelings were very strange. He turned round and round in the water like a wheel, strained his neck to look after them, and sent forth such a loud and strange cry, that it almost frightened himself. Ah! he could not forget them, those noble birds, those happy birds! The duckling knew not what the birds were called, knew not whither they were flying, yet he loved them as he had never before loved anything. He envied them not. It would never have occurred to him to wish such beauty for himself. He would have been quite

contented if the ducks in the duck-yard had but endured
his company.

And the winter was so cold, so cold! The duckling had
to swim round and round in the water, to keep it from
freezing. But every night the opening in which he swam
became smaller and smaller; the duckling had to make
good use of his legs to prevent the water from freezing
entirely. At last, wearied out, he lay stiff and cold in the
ice.

Early in the morning there passed by a peasant, who
saw him, broke the ice in pieces with his wooden shoes,
and carried the duckling home to his wife.

The duckling soon revived. The children would have
played with him, but he thought they wished to tease him,
and in his terror jumped into the milk-pail, so that the milk
was splashed about the room. The good woman screamed
and clapped her hands. He flew into the tub where first
the butter was kept, and thence into the meal-barrel, and
out again.

The woman screamed, and struck at him with the tongs;
the children ran races with each other trying to catch him,
and laughed and screamed likewise. It was well for him
that the door stood open; he jumped out among the bushes
into the new-fallen snow, and lay there as in a dream.

But it would be too sad to relate all the trouble and
misery he had to suffer during the winter. He was lying
on a moor among the reeds when the sun began to shine
warmly again. The larks were singing, and beautiful spring
had returned.

Once more he shook his wings. They were stronger than
formerly, and bore him forward quickly; and, before he
was well aware of it, he was in a large garden where the
apple-trees stood in full bloom, where the syringas sent
forth their fragrance, and hung their long green branches
down into the winding canal. Oh! everything was so
lovely, so full of the freshness of spring!

Out of the thicket came three beautiful white swans.
They displayed their feathers so proudly, and swam so

lightly, so lightly! The duckling knew the glorious creatures, and was seized with a strange sadness.

'I will fly to them, those kingly birds!' said he. 'They will kill me, because I, ugly as I am have presumed to approach them; but it matters not. Better be killed by them than be bitten by the ducks, pecked by the hens, kicked by the girl who feeds the poultry, and have so much to suffer during the winter!' He flew into the water, and swam towards the beautiful creatures. They saw him and shot forward to meet him. 'Only kill me,' said the poor duckling, and he bowed his head low, expecting death. But what did he see in the water? He saw beneath him his own form, no longer that of a plump, ugly grey bird— it was that of a swan!

It matters not to have been born in a duck-yard, if one has been hatched from a swan's egg.

The larger swans swam round him, and stroked him with their beaks, and he was very happy.

Some little children were running about in the garden. They threw grain and bread into the water, and the youngest exclaimed, 'There is a new one!' The others also cried out, 'Yes, a new swan has come!' and they clapped their hands, and ran and told their father and mother. Bread and cake were thrown into the water, and every one said, 'The new one is the best, so young, and so beautiful!' and the old swans bowed before him. The young swan felt quite ashamed, and hid his head under his wing. He was all too happy, but still not proud, for a good heart is never proud.

He remembered how he had been laughed at and cruelly treated, and he now heard every one say he was the most beautiful of all beautiful birds. The syringas bent down their branches towards him, and the sun shone warmly and brightly. He shook his feathers, stretched his slender neck, and in the joy of his heart said, 'How little did I dream of so much happiness when I was the ugly, despised duckling!'

THE NIGHTINGALE

The palace of the Emperor of China was the most beautiful palace in the world. It was made entirely of fine porcelain, which was so brittle that whoever touched it had to be very careful.

The choicest flowers were to be seen in the garden; and to the prettiest of these, little silver bells were fastened, in order that their tinkling might prevent any one from passing by without noticing them. Yes! everything in the Emperor's garden was wonderfully well arranged; and the garden itself stretched so far that even the gardener did not know the end of it. Whoever walked farther than the end of the garden, however, came to a beautiful wood with very high trees, and beyond that to the sea. The tall trees went down quite to the sea, which was very deep and blue, so that large ships could sail close under their branches; and among the branches dwelt a nightingale, who sang so sweetly that even the poor fishermen, who had so much else to do when they came out at night-time to cast their nets, would stand still to listen to her song.

Travellers came from all parts of the world to the Emperor's city, and they admired the city, the palace and the garden; but if they heard the nightingale they all said, 'This is the best.' And they talked about her after they went home, and learned men who wrote books about the city, the palace, and the garden, praised the nightingale above everything else. Poets also wrote the most beautiful verses about the nightingale of the wood near the sea.

These books went round the world, and one of them at last reached the Emperor. He read and read, and nodded his head every moment; for these splendid descriptions of the city, the palace, and the garden, pleased him greatly.

But at last he saw something that surprised him. The words 'But the nightingale is the best of all' were written in the book.

'What in the world is this?' said the Enperor. 'The nightingale! I do not know it at all! Can there be such a bird in my empire, in my garden even, without my having even heard of it? Truly one may learn something from books.'

So he called his Prime Minister. Now this was so grand a personage that no one of inferior rank might speak to him; and if one did venture to ask him a question, his only answer was 'Pooh!' which has no particular meaning.

'There is said to be a very remarkable bird here, called the nightingale,' began the Emperor; 'her song, they say, is worth more than anything else in all my dominions. Why has no one ever told me of her?'

'I have never before heard her mentioned,' said the Prime Minister; 'she has never been presented at court.'

'I wish her to come and sing before me this evening,' said the Emperor. 'The whole world, it seems, knows what I have, better than I do myself!'

'I have never before heard her mentioned,' said the Prime Minister, 'but I will seek her, and try to find her.'

But where was she to be found? The Prime Minister ran up one flight of steps, down another, through halls, and through passages, but not one of all the people he met had ever heard of the nightingale. So he went back to the Emperor, and said, 'It must be a fable invented by the man who wrote the book. Your Imperial Majesty must not believe all that is written in books; much in them is pure invention.'

'But the book in which I have read it,' said the Emperor, 'was sent me by the high and mighty Emperor of Japan, and therefore it cannot be untrue. I wish to hear the nightingale; she must be here this evening; and if she do not come, after supper the whole court shall be flogged.'

In great alarm, the Prime Minister again ran up stairs and down stairs, through halls and through passages; and half the court ran with him; for no one liked the idea of being flogged. Many were the questions asked about the wonderful nightingale, of whom the whole world talked, and about whom no one at court knew anything.

At last they met a poor little girl in the kitchen, who said, 'Oh yes! the nightingale! I know her very well. Oh! how she can sing! Every evening I carry the fragments left at table to my poor sick mother. She lives by the sea-shore; and when I am coming back, and stay to rest a little in the wood, I hear the nightingale sing. It makes the tears come into my eyes!'

'Little kitchen-maiden,' said the Prime Minister, 'I will get you a good place in the kitchen, and you shall have permission to see the Emperor dine, if you will take us to the nightingale; for she is expected at court this evening.'

So they went together to the wood where the nightingale was accustomed to sing, and half the court went with them. Whilst they were on the way, a cow began to low.

'Oh!' said the court pages, 'now we have her! It is certainly a wonderful voice for so small an animal; surely we have heard it somewhere before.'

'No, those are cows you hear lowing,' said the little kitchen-maid; 'we are still far from the place.'

The frogs were now croaking in the pond.

'There she is now!' said the chief court-preacher; 'her voice sounds just like little church-bells.'

'No, those are frogs,' said the little kitchen-maid, 'but we shall soon hear her.'

Then the nightingale began to sing.

'There she is!' said the little girl; 'listen! listen! There she sits,' she added, pointing to a little grey bird up in the branches.

'Is it possible?' said the Prime Minister. 'I should not have thought it. How simple she looks! She must certainly have changed colour at the sight of so many distinguished personages.'

'Little nightingale!' called out the kitchen-maid, 'our

gracious Emperor wishes you to sing something to him.'

'With the greatest pleasure,' said the nightingale, and she sang so beautifully that every one was enchanted.

'It sounds like glass bells,' said the Prime Minister. 'And look at her little throat, how it moves! It is singular that we should never have heard her before; she will have great success at court.'

'Shall I sing again to the Emperor?' asked the nightingale, for she thought the Emperor was among them.

'Most excellent nightingale!' said the Prime Minister, 'I have the honour to invite you to a court festival, which is to take place this evening, when His Imperial Majesty will be delighted to hear you sing.'

'My song would sound far better among the green trees,' said the nightingale; but she followed willingly when she heard that the Emperor wished it.

In the centre of the grand hall where the Emperor sat, a golden perch had been fixed, on which the nightingale was to sit. The whole court was present, and the little kitchen-maid received permission to stand behind the door, for she now had the rank and title of 'Maid of the Kitchen'. All were dressed in their finest clothes; and all eyes were fixed upon the little grey bird, to whom the Emperor nodded as a signal for her to begin.

The nightingale sang so sweetly that tears came into the Emperor's eyes and tears rolled down his cheeks. Then the nightingale sang more sweetly still, and touched the hearts of all who heard her; and the Emperor was so pleased that he said, 'The nightingale shall have my golden slippers, and wear them round her neck.' But the nightingale thanked him, and said she was already sufficiently rewarded.

'I have seen tears in the Emperor's eyes; that is the greatest reward I can have. The tears of an Emperor have a special value. I feel myself highly honoured.' And then she sang again more charmingly than ever.

'That singing is the most charming gift ever known,' said the ladies present; and they put water into their mouths, and tried when they spoke to move their throats as

*The nightingale sang so sweetly that tears came into
the Emperor's eyes*

she did. They thought to become nightingales also. Indeed, even the footmen and chamber-maids declared that they were quite satisfied; which was a great thing to say, for of all people they are the most difficult to please. Yes indeed! the nightingale's success was complete. She was now to remain at court, to have her own cage, with permission to fly out twice in the day and once in the night. Twelve servants were set apart to wait on her on these occasions, who were each to hold the end of a silken band fastened round her foot. There was not much pleasure in that kind of flying.

All the city was talking of the wonderful bird; and when two people met, one would say only 'nightin' and the other 'gale'; and then they sighed, and understood each other perfectly. Indeed, eleven of the children of the citizens were named after the nightingale; but not one of them could sing a note.

One day a large parcel arrived for the Emperor, on which was written 'The Nightingale'.

'Here we have another new book about our far-famed bird,' said the Emperor. But it was not a book; it was a little piece of mechanism lying in a box—an artificial nightingale, which was intended to look like the living one, but covered all over with diamonds, rubies, and sapphires. When this artificial bird had been wound up, it could sing one of the tunes that the real nightingale sang; and its tail, all glittering with silver and gold, went up and down all the time.

'That is splendid!' said every one; and he who had brought the bird was given the title of 'Chief Imperial Nightingale Bringer'.

Then the Emperor ordered that the real and the toy nightingales should sing together. But it did not succeed, for the real nightingale sang in her own natural way, and the artificial bird produced its tones by wheels.

'It is not his fault,' said the music master; 'he keeps exact time, and quite according to method.'

So the artificial bird now sang alone. He was quite as

successful as the real nightingale; and then he was so much
prettier to look at—his plumage sparkled like jewels.

Three and thirty times he sang one and the same tune,
and yet he was not weary. Every one would willingly have
heard him again. The Emperor, however, now wished the
real nightingale to sing something—but where was she?
No one had noticed that she had flown out of the open
window—flown away to her own green wood.

'What is the meaning of this?' said the Emperor; and
all the courtiers abused the nightingale, and called her a
most ungrateful creature. 'We have the best bird at all
events,' said they, and for the four and thirtieth time they
heard the same tune, but still they did not quite know it,
because it was so difficult. The music master praised the
bird very highly; indeed, he declared it was superior to
the real nightingale in every way.

'For see,' he said, 'with the real nightingale one could
never reckon on what was coming, but everything is settled
with the artificial bird. He will sing in this one way, and
no other. This can be proved; he can be taken to pieces,
and the works can be shown—where the wheels lie, how
they move, and just how one follows from another.'

'That is just what I think,' said everybody; and the
artist received permission to show the bird to the people
on the following Sunday. 'They too shall hear him sing,'
the Emperor said. So they heard him, and were as well
pleased as if they had all been drinking tea; for it is tea
that makes the Chinese merry. But the fisherman who had
heard the real nightingale, said, 'It sounds very pretty,
almost like the real bird; but yet there is something wanting,
I do not know what.'

The real nightingale was banished from the empire.

The artificial bird had his place on a silken cushion,
close to the Emperor's bed; all the presents he received,
gold and precious stones, lay around him. He had been
given the rank and title of 'High Imperial Toilet Singer'.

And the music master wrote five and twenty volumes
about the artificial bird, with the longest and most difficult

words that are to be found in the Chinese language. So, of course, all said they had read and understood them, otherwise they would have been stupid, and perhaps would have been flogged.

Thus it went on for a year. The Emperor, the court, and all the Chinese knew every note of the artificial bird's song by heart; but that was the very reason why they enjoyed it so much—they could now sing with him. The little boys in the street sang 'zizizi, cluck, cluck, cluck!' and the Emperor himself sang too.

But one evening, when the bird was in full voice and the Emperor lay in bed and listened, suddenly there was a 'whizz' inside the bird. Then a spring cracked.
'Whir-r-r-r' went all the wheels running round; and the music stopped.

The Emperor jumped quickly out of bed, and had his chief physician called; but of what use could he be? Then a clockmaker was fetched; and at last, after a great deal of discussion and consultation, the bird was in some measure put to rights again; but the clockmaker said he must be spared much singing, for the pegs were almost worn out, and it was impossible to put in new ones, at least without spoiling the music.

There was great lamentation, for now the artificial bird was allowed to sing only once a year, and even then there were difficulties. However, the music master made a short speech full of his favourite long words, and said the bird was as good as ever; and, of course, no one contradicted him.

When five years were passed away, a great affliction visited the whole empire, for the Emperor was ill, and it was reported that he could not live. A new Emperor had already been chosen, and the people stood in the street, outside the palace, and asked the Prime Minister how the Emperor was.

'Pooh!' said he, and shook his head.

Cold and pale lay the Emperor in his magnificent bed. All the court believed him to be already dead, and every one ran away to greet the new Emperor.

But the Emperor was not yet dead. He could scarcely breathe, however, and it appeared to him as though something was sitting on his chest. He opened his eyes, and saw that it was Death. He had put on the Emperor's crown, and in one hand held the golden scimitar and in the other the splendid imperial banner. From under the folds of the thick velvet hangings the strangest-looking heads were peering forth, some with very ugly faces, and others with looks that were extremely gentle and lovely. These were the bad and good deeds of the Emperor, which were now all fixing their eyes upon him, whilst Death sat on his heart.

'Do you know this?' they whispered one after another. 'Do you remember that?' And they began reproaching him in such a manner that the sweat broke out upon his forehead.

'I have never known anything like it,' said the Emperor. 'Music, music, the great Chinese drum!' cried he; 'let me not hear what they are saying.'

They went on, however; and Death, quite in the Chinese fashion, nodded his head to every word.

'Music, music!' cried the Emperor. 'You dear little golden bird! sing, I pray you, sing!—I have given you gold and precious stones. I have even hung my golden slippers round your neck—sing, I pray you, sing!'

But the bird was silent. There was no one there to wind him up; and without that he could not sing. Death continued to stare at the Emperor with his great hollow eyes! And everywhere it was still, fearfully still!

All at once came the sweetest music through the window. It was the little living nightingale who was sitting on a branch outside. She had heard of her Emperor's severe illness, and was come to sing to him of comfort and hope. As she sang, the spectral forms became paler and paler; the blood flowed more and more quickly through the Emperor's feeble members; and even Death listened, and said, 'Go on, little nightingale, go on.'

'Will you give me the beautiful golden sword? Will

you give me the rich banner? and will you give me the Emperor's crown?' said the bird.

And Death gave up all these treasures for a song. And the nightingale sang on. She sang of the quiet churchyard where white roses blossom, where the lilac sends forth its fragrance, and the fresh grass is bedewed with the tears of the sorrowing friends of the departed. Then Death was seized with a longing to see his garden, and, like a cold white shadow, flew out at the window.

'Thanks, thanks, little bird,' said the Emperor, 'I know you well. I banished you from my realm, and you have sung away those evil faces from my bed, and death from my heart. How can I reward you?'

'You have already rewarded me,' said the nightingale; 'I have seen tears in your eyes, as when I sang to you for the first time. Those I shall never forget; they are the jewels that gladden a minstrel's heart! But sleep now, and wake fresh and healthy. I will sing to you again.'

And she sang—and the Emperor fell into a sweet sleep. Oh, how soft and refreshing it was!

The sun shone in at the window when he awoke, strong and healthy. Not one of his servants had returned, for they all believed him dead; only the nightingale still sat beside him and sang.

'You shall always stay with me,' said the Emperor. 'You shall only sing when it pleases you, and the artificial bird I will break into a thousand pieces.'

'Do not so,' said the nightingale; 'he has done what he could; take care of him. I cannot stay in the palace; but let me come when I like. I will sit on the branches close to the window, in the evening, and sing to you, that you may become happy and have thoughts full of joy. I will sing to you of those who rejoice and of those who suffer. I will sing to you of all that is good or bad which is hidden from you. The little minstrel flies afar to the fisherman's hut, to the peasant's cottage, to all who are far distant from you and your court. I love your heart more than your crown, and yet the crown has an adour of something holy about it. I will come; I will sing. But you must promise me one thing.'

'Everything,' said the Emperor. And now he stood in his imperial splendour, which he had put on himself, and held to his heart the scimitar so heavy with gold.

'One thing I beg of you: let no one know that you have a little bird who tells you everything; then all will go on well.' And the nightingale flew away.

The attendants came in to look at their dead Emperor —and the Emperor said, 'Good-morning!'

THE TOP AND THE BALL

A top and a ball were lying together in a box, among other playthings, and the top said to the ball: 'Why should we not become bride and bridegroom, since we are thrown so much together?'

But the ball, who was made of morocco, and thought herself a very fine young lady, would not even condescend to answer.

The next day, the little boy to whom the playthings belonged came and painted the top red and yellow, and drove a brass nail into the middle of it, and then the top looked almost grand when he was spinning round. 'Look at me now!' said he to the ball; 'what do you say? Why should not we become man and wife? We suit each other so well. You can jump and I can spin; it would not be easy to find a couple happier than we should be.'

'Indeed!' said the ball. 'Perhaps you do not know that my father and mother were morocco slippers, and that I have a Spanish cork in my body.'

'Yes, but I am made of mahogany,' said the top. 'The Mayor made me with his own hands; for he has a lathe of his own, and took great pleasure in turning me.'

'Can I be sure of that?' said the ball.

'May I never be whipped again if I lie,' said the top. 'You can plead your cause very well,' said the ball; 'but I am not at liberty to accept your proposal. I am as good as engaged to a young swallow. Whenever I fly up in the air, he puts his head out of his nest and says: "Will you?" I have said "Yes" to him in my heart, and that is almost the same as being engaged. But I promise I will never forget you!'

'Much good that will be to me!' said the top; and they ceased speaking to each other.

Next day the ball was taken out. The top saw her fly up like a bird into the air, till she went quite out of sight. She came back, but every time she touched the ground she sprang higher than before. Either love, or the cork she had in her body, must have been the cause of this.

The ninth time she did not return, and though the boy sought and sought, he could not find her; she was gone.

'I know well where she is,' sighed the top; 'she is in the swallow's nest, and has married the swallow.' The more the top thought of her, the more beautiful did the ball appear. That she could not be his only made his love stronger. That she had liked another better than him was very sad. He could not forget that! And he span and hummed, but was always thinking of the dear ball, who in his memory grew more and more lovely. Thus years passed, and his was now an old love. He himself was no longer young! One day, however, he was gilded all over; never before had he looked so handsome. He was now a gilt top, and span most bravely, humming all the time. Yes, that was famous! But one day he sprang too high, and he, too, was gone! They sought and sought, even in the cellar; but he was nowhere to be found.

Where could he be? He had jumped into a barrel full of all sorts of rubbish—cabbage-stalks, sweepings, dust, and rain droppings that had fallen down from the gutter.

'Well, this is a nice place,' said he. 'My gay gilding will soon be spoiled here; and what sort of trumpery can I have fallen in with?' And he peeped at a long cabbage-stalk which lay fearfully near him, and at a strange round thing somewhat like an apple. But it was not an apple; it was an old ball that had lain for years in the gutter, and was quite soaked through.

'Thank goodness! At last I see an equal, with whom I may speak,' said the ball, looking fixedly at the gilt top. 'I am made of real morocco, sewed together by a young lady's hands, and I have Spanish cork in my body; though to see me now, no one would think so. I was on the point of marriage with the swallow when I fell into the gutter.

LITTLE IDA'S FLOWERS

'My flowers are quite faded,' said little Ida. 'Only yesterday evening they were so pretty, and now they are all drooping! What can be the reason of it?' asked she of the student who was sitting on the sofa. He was a great favourite with her, because he used to tell her stories, and cut out all sorts of pretty things for her in paper: hearts, and little ladies dancing in them; flowers; high castles with doors that could open. He was a charming student.

'Do you not know?' he asked. 'Your flowers went to a ball last night, and are tired; that is why they all hang their heads.'

'Surely flowers cannot dance!' cried little Ida.

'Of course they can dance!' said the student. 'When it is dark, and we are all gone to bed, they jump about as merrily as possible. They have a ball almost every night.'

'May children go to the ball too?' asked Ida.

'Yes,' said the student; 'daisies and lilies of the valley.'

'And where do the pretty flowers dance?' asked the child.

'Have you never been in the large garden in front of the King's beautiful summer palace, the garden so full of flowers?' said the student.

'I was there yesterday with my mother,' said Ida, 'but there were no leaves on the trees, neither did I see a single flower. What could have become of them? There were so many in the summer-time!'

'They are now in the palace,' answered the student. 'As soon as the King leaves his summer abode, and returns with all his court to the town, the flowers also hasten out of the garden and into the palace, where they enjoy themselves very much. Oh! if you could but see them! The two loveliest roses sit on the throne, and act King and

Queen. The red cockscombs then arrange themselves in rows before them, bowing very low. These are the gentlemen of the bedchamber. After that the prettiest among the flowers come in, and open the ball. The blue violets are for little naval cadets, and they begin dancing with the hyacinths and crocuses, who take the part of young ladies. The tulips and the tall orange-lilies are old dowagers, whose business it is to see that everything goes on with perfect propriety.'

'But,' asked little Ida, 'may the flowers when they choose give their ball in the King's palace?'

'No one knows anything about it,' replied the student. 'Perhaps once during the night the old chamberlain may come in, with his great bunch of keys, to see that all is right; but as soon as the flowers hear the clanking of the keys they are quite still, and hide themselves behind the long silken window curtains. 'I smell flowers here,' says the old chamberlain, but he is not able to find them.'

'That is very funny,' said Ida, clapping her little hands; 'but could not I see the flowers?'

'To be sure you could!' answered the student. 'You have only to peep in at the window next time you go to the palace. I did so today, and saw a long yellow lily lying on the sofa. That was a court lady.'

'Can the flowers in the Botanic Garden go there too?' asked Ida. 'Can they go so far?'

'Certainly, for flowers can fly if they wish,' replied he. 'The pretty red and yellow butterflies, that look so much like flowers, are in fact nothing else. They jump from their stalks, move their petals as if they were little wings, and fly about. As a reward for always behaving themselves well, they are allowed, instead of sitting quietly on their stalks, to flutter hither and thither all day long, till wings actually grow out of their petals. It may be that the flowers in the Botanic Garden have not heard what merry-making goes on every night at the palace; but I assure you, if, next time you go into the garden, you whisper to one of the flowers that a ball is to be given at night at the castle, the news will be repeated from flower to flower, and thither they will all fly. Then, should the professor come into the garden and find all his flowers gone, he will wonder what is become of them.'

'Indeed!' said Ida. 'But how can the flowers repeat to each other what I say to them? I am sure flowers cannot speak.'

'No, they cannot speak, you are right there,' answered the student; 'but they make themselves understood by signs. Have you never seen them move to and fro at the least breath of air? In that they can understand each other as well as we can by talking.'

'And does the professor understand their signs?' asked Ida.

'Certainly!' said the student. 'One morning he came into the garden, and saw a tall nettle was making signs to a pretty red carnation. 'You are so beautiful,' it was saying, 'and I love you so much!' But the professor could not allow such things, so clapped his hands on the nettle's leaves, which as you know, are its fingers, and the leaves stung him sharply, and since then he has never dared to touch a nettle.'

'Ha, ha!' laughed little Ida, 'that was funny.'

'What do you mean,' said a tiresome lawyer, who had come on a visit and was sitting on the sofa, 'by putting such things into children's heads?' He could not bear the student, and always used to scold when he saw him cutting out funny figures—as, for instance, a man on the gallows holding a heart in his hand, meant for a heart-stealer; or an old witch riding on a broomstick and carrying her husband on the tip of her nose. The lawyer did not like these jokes, and used to say as he had just said, 'How can any one put such nonsense into a child's head? What silly fancies they are!'

But little Ida thought what the student had told her about the flowers was very wonderful, and she could not leave off thinking of it. She was now sure that her flowers hung their heads because they were tired with dancing so much the night before. So she took them to the pretty little table in her room where her playthings lay. Her doll lay sleeping in the cradle, but Ida said to her, 'You must get up, Sophy, and be content to sleep tonight in the table-drawer, for the poor flowers are ill, and must sleep in your bed; perhaps they will be well again by tomorrow.' She then took out the doll, who said not a word but looked vexed and cross at having to give up her cradle to the flowers.

Ida then laid the flowers in the doll's bed, drew the quilt over them, and told them to lie quite still whilst she made some tea for them, so that they might be quite well again the next day. And she drew the curtains round the bed, so that the sun might not dazzle their eyes.

All the evening she thought of nothing but the student's words; and just before she went to bed she ran up to the window, where her mother's tulips and hyacinths stood behind the blinds, and whispered to them, 'I know very well that you are going to a ball tonight.' But the flowers moved not a leaf, and seemed not to have heard her.

After she was in bed she thought for a long time how delightful it must be to see the flowers dancing in the King's palace; and she said to herself, 'I wonder whether my flowers have been there?' And while she was wondering she fell asleep. During the night she awoke. She had been dreaming of the student and the flowers, and of the lawyer who told her that the student was making game of her. All was still in the room, the night-lamp was burning on the table, and her father and mother were both asleep.

'I wonder whether my flowers are still in Sophy's bed?' said she. 'I should very much like to know.' She raised herself a little, and looking towards the door, which stood half open, she saw that the flowers and all her playthings were just as she had left them. She listened, and it seemed to her as if some one must be playing on the piano; but the tones were lower and sweeter than any she had ever heard before.

'Now my flowers must certainly be dancing in there,' she thought. 'Oh, how I should like to see them!' But she dared not get up for fear of waking her father and mother. 'If they would only come in here!' But the flowers did not come, and the piano sounded so sweetly. At last she could bear it no longer. She must see the dancing. So she crept lightly out of bed, and stole towards the door of the room. Oh, what wonderful things she saw then!

No night-lamp was burning; but it was quite light in the room, for the moon shone through the window, upon the floor. All the hyacinths and tulips stood there in two rows, whilst their empty pots might still be seen in front of the windows. The flowers were dancing gracefully, holding each other by their long green leaves as they turned round. At the piano sat a large yellow lily, which Ida felt sure she must have seen before, for she remembered the student saying that this flower was very much like Miss Laura, one of Ida's friends; and how every one had laughed. Now she herself saw that the lily was very like her friend, for it had exactly her way of playing, bowing its long yellow face now to one side, now to the other, and nodding its head to mark the time. A tall blue crocus now stepped forward, sprang upon the table on which lay Ida's playthings, went straight up to the bed, and drew back the curtains. There lay the sick flowers; but they got up at once and greeted the other flowers, who invited them to dance with them. The sick flowers looked quite well again, and danced as merrily as the rest.

Suddenly a noise, as of something falling from the table, was heard. Ida cast a glance that way, and saw that it was the rod which she had found on her bed on the morning of Shrove Tuesday, and which seemed desirous of taking its place among the flowers. It was certainly a very pretty rod, and a little wax doll was fixed on the top of it, wearing a hat as broad-brimmed as the lawyer's, with a blue and red ribbon tied round it. The rod hopped about in the middle of the flowers and stamped the floor merrily. It was dancing the Mazurka, which the flowers could not dance because they were so light-footed.

All at once the wax doll on the rod swelled out to a giant,

tall and broad, and exclaimed in a loud voice, 'How can any one put such nonsense into a child's head? What silly fancies they are!' And now the doll looked as much like the lawyer in his broad-brimmed hat as one drop of water looks like another. Its face looked as yellow and peevish as his. The paper flowers on the rod, however, pinched its thin legs, whereupon it shrunk up and was again a little wax doll. Little Ida thought this scene so droll that she could not help laughing. The company, however, did not notice it, for the rod continued to stamp about, and the doll-lawyer was obliged to dance, too, whether he would or not, and make himself now thin, now thick, now tall, now short, till at last the flowers interceded for him, and the rod then left him in piece.

A loud knocking was now heard from the drawer in which lay Ida's doll. It was Sophy who made the noise. She put her head out of the drawer and asked in great astonishment, 'Is there a ball here? Why has no one told me of it?'

'Will you dance with me?' asked the nut-crackers.

'Certainly you are a very fit person to dance with me!' said Sophy, turning her back to him. She then sat down on the table, expecting that one of the flowers would come and ask her to dance, but no one came. She coughed—'Hem! hem!'—still no one came. Meantime the nut-crackers danced by himself.

As no flowers came forward to ask Sophy to dance, all at once she let herself fall down on the floor, which made a great noise, and all the flowers ran up to ask her whether she had hurt herself. Fortunately she was not at all hurt. The flowers were now all very polite, especially Ida's flowers, who thanked her for the nice bed in which they had slept. Then they led her into the middle of the room where the moon shone and danced with her, whilst all the other flowers stood in a circle round them. Sophy was now quite happy, and begged Ida's flowers to make use of her bed again after the ball, as she did not at all mind sleeping one night in the table-drawer.

But the flowers said, 'We owe you many thanks for

your kindness, but we shall not live long enough to need it; we shall be quite dead by tomorrow. Still, please ask little Ida to bury us in the garden near her canary-bird; then next summer we shall wake again and be even more beautiful than we have been this year.'

'No, you must not die!' replied Sophy, as she kissed the flowers.

Just then the door was suddenly opened, and a number of flowers danced in. Ida could not understand where these flowers came from, unless from the King's Garden. First came two lovely roses wearing golden crowns. These were the King and Queen. Then followed stocks and pinks, bowing to all who were present. They had also a band with them. Great poppies and peonies blew upon the shells of peas till they were quite red in the face, whilst blue and white campanulas rang a merry peal on their bells. Then came a great many other flowers: violets, daisies, lilies of the valley, narcissuses, and others, who all moved so gracefully that it was delightful to see them.

At last, these happy flowers wished one another 'Good-night'; and little Ida crept into bed to dream of all the beautiful things she had seen.

Next morning, as soon as she was dressed, she went to her little table to see if her flowers were there. She drew aside the bed-curtains—yes! there lay the flowers, but they were today much more faded than yesterday. Sophy too was lying in the drawer, but she looked very sleepy.

'Do you remember what the flowers told you to say to me?' asked little Ida. But Sophy looked stupid, and did not say a word.

'You are not at all good!' said Ida, 'and yet all the flowers let you dance with them.' She then chose out from her playthings a little pasteboard box with birds painted on it, and in it she placed the faded flowers. 'That shall be your coffin,' said she, 'and when my cousins come to see me, they shall go with me to bury you in the garden, in order that next summer you may bloom again, and be still more beautiful than you have been this year.'

The two cousins of whom she spoke were two lively boys, called James and Adolphus. Their father had given them two new cross-bows, which they brought with them to show to Ida. She then told them of the poor flowers that were dead, and were to be buried in the garden. The two boys walked in front with their bows slung across their shoulders, and little Ida followed carrying the dead flowers in their pretty coffin. A grave was dug for them in the garden. Ida kissed the flowers once more, then laid the box down in the hollow, and James and Adolphus shot arrows over the grave with their cross-bows, for they had neither guns nor cannon.

THE SANDMAN

There is no one in the whole world who knows so many stories as the Sandman, or who can tell them so well.

In the evening, when children are sitting quietly at table, or on their little stools, he takes off his shoes, comes softly upstairs, opens the door very gently, and throws sand in their eyes; just enough to hinder the children from keeping them open and seeing him. He then glides behind them, and breathes lightly, very lightly, upon their necks, and thereupon their heads become very heavy. But it does them no harm, for the Sandman means it kindly. He only wants the children to be quiet, and they are never quiet but when they are in bed and asleep. They must be quiet, that he may tell them his stories.

When the children are asleep, the Sandman sits down upon the bed. He is gaily dressed; his coat is of silk, but of what colour it is impossible to say, for it seems now green, now red, now blue, according to the light. Under each arm he carries an umbrella. One, which has pictures painted on it, he holds over good children, and then they have the most delightful dreams all night long; and the other, which has nothing on it, he holds over naughty children, so that they sleep heavily, and awake in the morning without having dreamed at all.

Now let us hear what stories the Sandman told to a little boy named Hialmar, to whom he came every evening for a whole week.

MONDAY

'Listen to me,' said the Sandman, as soon as he had got Hialmar into bed, 'and I will decorate your room.' While he was speaking, the flowers in the flower-pots grew up into large trees, whose long branches stretched to the ceiling and spread along the walls, so that the room looked like a beautiful arbour. All the branches were laden with flowers, every flower more beautiful even than the rose, and more fragrant. Moreover, could you have tasted them you would have found them sweeter than sugar. Fruit, which shone like gold, hung from the trees, and dumplings full of currants. Never was the like seen before. But, at the same time, a loud wailing was heard in the table-drawer, where Hialmar's school-books were kept.

'What is the matter?' said the Sandman, going up to the table, and taking out the drawer. There lay the slate, on which the figures were pressing and squeezing together, because a wrong figure had got into the sum, so that it was near falling to pieces. The pencil hopped and skipped about like a little dog; he wanted to help the sum, but he could not. And a little farther off lay Hialmar's copy-book. At the beginning of every line on each page stood a large letter with a little letter by its side; this was the copy. And after them stood other letters intended to look like the copy. Hialmar had written these; but they seemed to have fallen over the lines, upon which they ought to have stood.

'Look, this is the way you must hold yourselves,' said the copy; 'look, slanting just so, and turning round with a jerk.'

'Oh! we would do so willingly,' said Hialmar's letters; 'but we cannot, we are so badly made!'

'Then you shall have some of the children's physic,' said the sandman.

'Oh no!' cried they, and stood so straight that it was a pleasure to see them.

'Well, I cannot tell you any more stories now,' said the Sandman; 'I must drill these letters: right, left, right, left!' So he drilled the letters till they looked as straight and perfect as only the letters in a copy can be. However, when Hialmar looked at them the next morning, they were as miserable and badly formed as before.

TUESDAY

As soon as Hialmar was in bed, the Sandman touched with his magic wand all the pieces of furniture in the room. Thereupon they all began to chatter, and each piece talked only about itself, excepting the spittoon, who stood quite still, and was much vexed at their being so vain, all chattering about themselves, without ever thinking of him, who stood so modestly in the corner and suffered himself to be spat upon.

Over the chest of drawers hung a large picture in a gilt frame. The picture was a landscape showing tall old trees, flowers blossoming in the grass, and a river that wound its way through the wood and past many a grand old castle till it reached the sea.

The Sandman touched the picture with his magic wand; and immediately the birds began to sing, the branches waved to and fro, and the clouds sailed by, casting their shadows over the fields below.

The Sandman then lifted little Hialmar up to the frame, and put his feet into the picture. There he stood amid the tall grass. He ran to the water's edge, and sat down in a little boat that was painted red and white and had sails glittering like silver. Six swans, with golden wreaths round their necks and bright blue stars upon their heads, drew the boat along close to a green wood, where the trees were telling stories about robbers and witches, and the flowers were talking of the pretty little fairies, and of what the butterflies had said to them.

Lovely fishes, with scales like gold and silver, swam behind the boat, every now and then leaping up so that the water was splashed over Hialmar's head; birds red and blue, great and small, flew after him in two long rows; the gnats danced, and the cockchafers sang 'Boom, boom' They all wished to go with Hialmar, and every one of them had a story to tell.

A pleasant voyage that was. The woods were now close

and dark; now like beautiful gardens beaming with flowers and sunshine. Large palaces built of glass and marble rose from among the trees; and on the balconies stood young princesses. These were all little girls whom Hialmar knew well, and with whom he had often played. They stretched out their hands to him, each holding a pretty little heart made of sugar, such as is seen in confectioners' shops. Hialmar seized the end of one of these little hearts as he sailed by, and a princess kept hold of the other, so each got half—the princess the smaller, Hialmar the larger. At every castle gate a little prince was keeping guard. Each shouldered a golden scimitar, and showered down raisins and tin soldiers. You could see at once that these were true princes. Hialmar sailed sometimes through woods, sometimes through lofty halls, or through busy towns. He sailed through the town where the nurse lived who had cared for him when he was a baby, and who loved him so much. She nodded and beckoned to him as he passed by, and sang the song she herself had written and sent to him—

> Beloved Hialmar, my baby dear,
> My constant thoughts on thee attend:
> On cheeks, and mouth, and eyes so clear
> I shower my kisses without end.
>
> With joy your first lisped word I heard,
> And now to thee Adieu must say.
> May God my nursling angel guard
> In every hour; I fondly pray.

And all the birds sang with her, the flowers danced upon their stalks, and the old trees nodded their heads whilst the Sandman told stories to them also.

WEDNESDAY

How the rain was pouring down! Hialmar could hear it even in his sleep, and when the Sandman opened the window the water came up to the window-sill. There was

At every castle gate a little prince was keeping guard

quite a lake in front of the house, and on it a lovely ship.

'Will you sail with me, little Hialmar?' said the Sand-man. 'If you will, you shall visit foreign lands tonight, and be here again by the morning.'

And now Hialmar, dressed in his Sunday clothes, was in the ship. The weather cleared up at once, and they floated down the street, round the church, and were soon sailing upon the wide rolling sea. They quickly lost sight of land, and could see only a flight of storks, who had left their own country and were going to a warmer one. The storks were flying one after another, and had already been flying a long time. One of them was so weary that his wings could scarcely bear him up any longer. He was the last of the row, and was soon far behind the others. He sank lower and lower, with his wings outspread. He still tried to move them, but it was all in vain. His wings touched the ship's cordage, he slid down the sail, and—crash! there he stood on the deck.

So the cabin-boy caught him and put him where the hens, and ducks, and turkeys were kept. The poor stork stood amongst them quite dazed.

'Only look, what a foolish fellow!' said all the hens. And the turkey-cock made himself as big as he could, and asked him who he was; and the ducks waddled backwards and cried 'Quack, quack!'

The stork then told them about warm Africa, about the pyramids, and about the ostrich, who races across the desert like a wild horse; but the ducks did not understand him, and quacked to each other, 'Isn't he very stupid?'

'Yes, indeed he is stupid!' said the turkey-cock, and began to gobble.

So the stork was silent, and thought of Africa. 'You have really very pretty slender legs!' said the turkey-cock. 'What did they cost you a yard?'

'Quack, quack, quack,' all the ducks began to titter; but the stork seemed not to have heard the question.

'You might just as well have laughed with them,' said the turkey-cock to him. 'It was a capital joke! But perhaps it was too deep for you? Ah! ah! isn't he clever? Let us have some fun while he is here.' And then he gobbled, the hens cackled, and the ducks quacked. What a dreadful noise they made with their fun!

But Hialmar went to the hen-house, opened the door, and called the stork, who at once jumped on deck. He had now rested himself and he looked happy, and nodded his head to Hialmar, as if to thank him. He then spread his wings and flew away—whilst the hens cackled, the ducks quacked, and the turkey-cock turned red as fire.

'Tomorrow, we will have you all made into soup!' said Hialmar; whereupon he awoke, and found himself in his own little bed. A strange journey had the Sandman taken that night!

THURSDAY

'I'll tell you what!' said the Sandman, 'do not be afraid, and you shall see a little mouse!' Then he held out his hand, with the pretty little animal in it. 'She is come to invite you to a wedding; there are two little mice here, who intend this very night to be married. They live under the floor of the dining-room, so theirs must be a pretty house.'

'But how can I get through the little hole?' asked Hialmar.

'Let me take care of that,' said the Sandman. 'I will make you very little!' and he touched Hialmar with his magic wand, and he became smaller and smaller, till at last he was no larger than his own fingers. 'Now, you can borrow the tin soldier's clothes; I think they will just fit you; and it looks so grand to wear uniform when you are in company.'

'Ah yes!' said Hialmar, and in another moment he was dressed like the prettiest little tin soldier.

'Will you be so good as to sit down in your mother's thimble?' said the little mouse, 'and I shall have the pleasure of drawing you to the wedding.'

'Will your ladyship really take so much trouble?' said Hialmar. And away they went to the mouse's wedding.

They first came to a long passage under the floor, just high enough for the thimble to be drawn along through it. It was lighted throughout with toadstools.

'Is there not a pleasant smell here?' said the mouse who was drawing the thimble. 'The passage has been smeared with rind bacon. There is nothing more delightful!'

They now entered the bridal hall. The lady mice stood on the right hand, whispering together, seemingly very merry; on the left side stood the gentlemen mice stroking their whiskers with their paws. In the middle of the room, in the scooped-out rind of a cheese, the bride and bridegroom were standing kissing each other before the eyes of all present. The whole room, like the passage, was smeared with the rind of bacon. This was all the entertainment given. For dessert, however, a pea was brought out, in which a little mouse belonging to the family had bitten the initials of the married couple. Was not this a splendid idea?

All the mice said that it had been a very nice wedding, and that they had had a very happy evening.

When it was all over, Hialmar returned home. He had certainly been in most distinguished company; but still, he felt as though he had rather lowered himself by becoming so small and wearing the uniform of a tin soldier.

FRIDAY

'What are we to do tonight?' asked Hialmar.

'Why, I do not know whether you would like to go to another wedding?' said the Sandman. 'The one of which I am now speaking is quite different from yesterday's. Your sister's big doll, that looks like a man and is called Herman, is going to marry the doll Bertha. It is also Bertha's birthday; so they will doubtless receive a great many presents.'

'Oh yes! I know that already,' said Hialmar, 'Whenever the dolls want new clothes, my sister calls it either their birthday or their wedding-day. They must certainly have been married a hundred times already.'

'Yes, but tonight they will be married for the hundred and first time; and when that is over they can never be married again. So this time the wedding will be a very grand affair indeed. Only look!'

Hialmar looked at the table, where stood the little doll's house. The windows were lighted up, and tin soldiers presented arms at the door. The bride and bridegroom were sitting on the floor leaning against the leg of the table. The Sandman put on Hialmar's grandmother's black gown and married them. When the ceremony was over, all the furniture in the room began singing a pretty song which had been written by the lead-pencil and went to the tune of the drummer's tattoo:—

> Our joyous chorus cast to the blast;
> Now all forms are past, they are fast.
> Hurrah! for bridal pair, both so fair;
> Both made of leather rare, past compare;
> And though both deaf and blind, never mind;
> Ring forth our greetings kind, on the wind.

And now presents were brought to them. All eatables, however, they declined; love was enough for them to live upon.

'Shall we go to the country, or make a tour in some foreign land?' asked the bridegroom. So the swallow, who had travelled a good deal, and the old hen, who had hatched five broods of chickens, were consulted. And the swallow spoke of those beautiful, warm countries where bunches of grapes, large and heavy, hang on the vines; where the air is so balmy, and the mountains of various hues, such as are never known here.

'But then they have not our green cabbages!' said the hen. 'One summer, I and all my chickens lived in the country. There was a gravel-pit, in which we might go and scrape about, and we had access to a garden that was full of green cabbages. Oh, how green they were! I cannot imagine anything more beautiful!'

'But one cabbage looks exactly like another,' said the swallow; 'and then we so often have wet weather here.'

'One gets accustomed to that,' said the hen.

'But it is so cold, it freezes.'

'That is good for the cabbages,' said the hen. 'But it can be warm sometimes. Did we not, four years ago, have a summer which lasted five weeks? It was so hot that one could hardly breathe. Then, too, in this country, we have no poisonous animals and we are free from robbers. He is a blockhead who does not think our country the most beautiful of all! he does not deserve to live here!' At these words, tears rolled down the hen's cheeks. 'I too have travelled; I have been twelve miles in a coop. There is no pleasure at all in travelling.'

'Yes, the hen is a sensible animal!' said the doll Bertha. 'I do not wish to travel over the mountains. It is only going up to come down again. No, we will go to the gravel-pit and walk in the garden among the cabbages.'

And so it was settled.

SATURDAY

'Now may I have some stories?' asked little Hialmar as soon as the Sandman had put him to sleep.

'We shall have no time for them this evening,' said the Sandman, spreading his picture umbrella over him. 'Look at these Chinese!' The umbrella resembled a large Chinese plate, with blue trees and pointed bridges on which little Chinese men and women stood nodding their heads.

'By tomorrow morning all the world must be made fine,' said the Sandman, 'it is a festival day, it is Sunday. I must go to the church-tower, to see whether the little spirits of the church are rubbing the bells so as to make them sound sweetly. I must away to the fields, to see that the winds are sweeping the dust off the grass and leaves. I must take down the stars, also, to brighten them. I put them into my apron; but first they must be numbered, and the holes in which they sit, up in the sky, must be numbered also, so that every one may return to his proper place; else they would not sit firmly, and we should have too many falling stars.'

'Listen to me, Mr. Sandman,' said an old portrait which hung on the wall, near the bed. 'Do you know that I am Hialmar's great-grandfather? I am much obliged to you for telling the boy stories; but you must not puzzle him. Stars cannot be taken down and brightened; they are bodies like our earth.'

'Many thanks, old great-grandfather!' said the Sandman, 'many thanks! You are certainly very old, but I am older still. I know how to behave myself to high and low. Now you may tell the stories yourself.' So the Sandman walked off, taking his umbrella with him.

'Well, I never!' said the portrait. 'Dare one not even express an opinion nowadays?' Then Hialmar awoke.

SUNDAY

'Good evening!' said the Sandman; and Hialmar nodded his head to him, and jumped up to turn his great-grandfather's portrait to the wall, in order that it might not interrupt him as it did yesterday.

'Now you shall tell me stories about the five green peas that all lived in one pod, and about the chickseed courting the chickweed, and about the darning-needle that wished to be fashionable and fancied herself a fine needle.'

'One may have too much of a good thing,' said the Sandman. 'I would rather show you something else; I will show you my brother. He never comes more than once to any one; and whomsoever he visits, he takes on his horse, and tells him a story. He knows only two stories;

the one more delightful than any one in the world can imagine; the other so dreadful, it cannot be described.' And the Sandman lifted little Hialmar up to the window, saying, 'There is my brother, the other Sandman. He is also called Death! You see he is not so frightful as he is shown in picture-books, where he seems to be all bones. No, he wears clothes embroidered with silver; a mantle of black velvet flies over his horse, behind him. See how he gallops!'

And Hialmar saw the other Sandman ride on, and take old and young with him on his horse. Some he placed in front, and others behind; but he always asked first what sort of mark-book they had to show.

'Good,' they all replied. 'Yes, but let me see it,' said he. So they were obliged to show it to him; and all those who had 'Very Good' written in it were put in front of the horse, and heard the story that was so delightful. But those who had 'Pretty Good' or 'Bad' in their mark-book were made to get up behind, and listen to the dreadful story. They trembled and wept; they tried to jump down from the horse's back, but that they could not, for they were as firmly fixed on it as if they had grown there.

'Death is a most beautiful Sandman,' said Hialmar. 'I am not afraid of him.'

'That you should not be,' said the Sandman, 'only take care to have a good mark-book to show.'

'This is very instructive,' muttered the grandfather's portrait. 'It's always good to give one's opinion.'

These are the stories of the Sandman; perhaps he may tell you more this very evening.

THUMBYKIN

Once upon a time there was a woman who wished very much for a little child, but did not know where to find one. So at last she went to a witch and said to her: 'I do so much wish to have a little child; can you, who are so wise, tell me where I can find one?'

'I can readily do so,' said the witch. 'There is nothing easier. Here is a barley corn, but it is quite unlike those that grow in the farmers' fields and that the fowls eat. Put it into a flower-pot and wait and see what takes place.'

'Oh, thank you so much,' said the woman, giving the witch twelve shillings, which was the price she asked for her barley corn. Thereafter she went straight home and planted the barely corn, and at once a large handsome flower sprang up. It looked something like a tulip, but its leaves were as tightly closed as if they were the leaves of a bud. 'What a lovely flower!' said the woman, kissing its red and golden coloured leaves. At her kiss the leaves burst open with a crack and she saw that it was really a tulip such as one can see almost anywhere. But lo! in the very centre of the blossom, on one of the green velvet stamens, sat a tiny maiden, a delicate and graceful little creature, scarcely half as long as a thumb; and when the woman saw her she called her Thumbykin, because she was so small.

A finely polished walnut shell formed her cradle, and therein, on a bed of violets, under a rose-leaf coverlet, Thumbykin slept soundly at night. During the day she amused herself by floating across a plate full of water in a large tulip-leaf which served her for a boat. The woman had placed the plate of water on a table, and put a wreath of flowers round the edge of it, and from side to side of the plate the little maiden rowed herself with two oars made of white horse-hair. It was pretty to see her and prettier still to hear her singing in a voice as clear as a tiny silver bell. Such singing certainly had never before been heard.

One night as she lay asleep in her pretty little bed, a large ugly old toad crept through a broken pane in the window and leapt up on the table. 'What a lovely little creature this is!' she thought, 'and what a charming wife she would make for my son!' So she took up the walnut shell in which the little maiden lay asleep under her coverlet of rose-leaf, and leapt with it through the window, and so hopped back again into the garden.

Now through the garden a broad stream flowed, and in its marshy banks the old toad lived with her son. He was uglier even than his mother, and when he saw the pretty little maiden in her beautiful bed he was able only in his harsh voice to cry, 'Croak, croak, croak.'

'Don't make such a noise,' said the old toad, 'or you will wake her and then she may fly away, for she is as light as thistledown. We will put her on one of the large water-lily leaves that grow in the middle of the stream. It will seem an island to her; she is so small. She will not be able to get away from it, and we shall have plenty of time to get the state-room under the marsh, where you are to live when you are married.'

Out in the middle of the stream grew a number of water-lilies, with broad green leaves that floated on the top of the water. The largest of these leaves seemed much farther off than any of the rest, and thither the old toad swam, carrying with her the walnut shell in which Thumbykin still lay sound asleep.

Very early in the morning the poor little creature awoke, and when she saw where she was she began to cry bitterly, for all round the leaf on which she was there was water, and she could see no way of ever reaching the land.

Meanwhile, down in the marsh the old toad was as busy as possible decking out her room with sedge and yellow rushes, so as to make it pretty and comfortable for her new daughter-in-law. When she had finished her work she swam out with her ugly son to the leaf where she had placed poor Thumbykin. She wished to carry off the pretty bed, that she might put it in the bridal chamber to be ready for the bride. To the little maiden the old toad in the water bowed low and said, 'Here is my son. He is to be your husband, and you will have a very happy life together in the fine house I have prepared for you down in the marsh by the stream.'

'Croak, croak, croak,' was all the ugly son could say for himself.

So the old toad and her son took up the pretty little cradle and swam away with it, leaving Thumbykin sitting weeping all alone on the green lily-leaf. She could not bear to think of living all alone with the old toad, and of having her ugly son for a husband.

Now the little fishes, who had been swimming about in the water, and had seen the old toad and had heard every word she said, leaped up till their heads were above the water, so that they might see the little girl; and when they caught sight of her they saw that she was very pretty, and they felt very sorry that any one so pretty should have to go and live with the ugly toads.

'No, no!' said they. 'Such a thing must never be allowed.'

So all the little fishes gathered together in the water round the green stalk of the leaf on which the little maiden stood, and they bit the stalk with their teeth until at last they bit it through. Then away went the leaf sailing quickly down the stream, and carrying Thumbykin far away where the toad could never reach her.

Past many towns she sailed, and when the birds in the bushes saw her they sang, 'What a lovely little girl!' On floated the leaf, carrying her farther and farther away, until at last she came to another land. Round her head a pretty little white butterfly kept constantly fluttering, till at last it settled on the leaf. He was greatly pleased with Thumbykin, and she was glad of it, for it was not possible now that the ugly toad could ever reach her, and the land through which she was sailing was very beautiful, and the sun shone on the water till it glowed and sparkled like silver. So Thumbykin took off her sash and tied one end of it round the butterfly, and fixed the other end to the leaf, which now sped on much faster than before, having the butterfly for a sail and took the little maiden with it.

Presently a great cockchafer flew past. The moment he caught sight of the maiden he seized her, putting his claws round her slim waist, and away he flew with her into a tree. But the green leaf floated on down the river, and the butterfly flew with it; for he was tied to the leaf, and could not get away.

Oh, how frightened Thumbykin was when the cockchafer flew away with her into the tree! She was sorry, too, for the pretty white butterfly which she had tied to the leaf; for, if he could not free himself, he would certainly die of hunger. But the cockchafer did not worry himself about that. He sat down beside her on one of the leaves of the tree, and gave her some honey from a flower to eat, and told her that she was very pretty, though not at all like a cockchafer. In a little all the cockchafers that lived in the tree came to visit her. They stared their hardest at Thumbykin, and one young lady cockchafer said, 'Why, she has only two legs! How ugly that looks!' 'She has no feelers,' said another; 'how stupid she must be!' 'How slender her waist is!' said a third. 'Pooh! she looks just like a human being.'

'How ugly she is!' said all the lady cockchafers. Thumbykin was really very lovely, and the cockchafer who had carried her off thought so; but when they all said she was ugly, he began to think that it must be true. So he would have nothing more to say to Thumbykin, but told her that she might go where she pleased. Then the cockchafers flew down with her from the tree, and placed her on a daisy, and Thumbykin wept because she thought she was so ugly that the cockchafers would have nothing to say to her. And all the time she was in reality one of the loveliest creatures in the world, and as tender and delicate as a rose-leaf.

All the summer through poor Thumbykin lived all alone in the forest. She wove for herself a little bed with blades of grass, and she hung it up under a clover-leaf so that she might be sheltered from the rain. For food she sucked the honey from the flowers, and from the leaves every morning she drank the dew. So the summer and the autumn passed away, and then came the long cold winter. The birds that had sung to her so sweetly had all flown away; the trees had lost their leaves, and the flowers were withered. The great clover-leaf under whose shelter she had lived was now rolled together and shrivelled up, and nothing of it was left but a yellow withered stalk.

Poor Thumbykin felt very, very cold, for her clothes were torn, and she was such a frail, delicate little thing that she nearly died. The snow, too, began to fall, and each flake, as it fell on her, was like a whole shovelful falling on one of us; for we are tall, and she was only about an inch high. Then she rolled herself up in a dry leaf; but it cracked in the middle, and there was no warmth in it, so she shivered with cold. Very near the wood in which she had been living there was a large corn-field, but the corn had been cut long before this, and there was nothing left but the hard, dry stubble standing up out of the frozen ground. To Thumbykin, going through it, it was like struggling through another forest; and, oh, how bitterly cold it was! At last she came to the door of the house of a field-mouse, who lived in a hole under the stubble. It was a warm, cosy house, and the mouse was very happy, for she had a whole roomful of corn, besides a kitchen and a fine dining-room. Poor little Thumbykin stood before the door of the house, just like a beggar girl, and prayed the mouse for a small bit of barley corn, because she was starving, having had nothing to eat for the last two days.

'Poor little thing!' said the field-mouse, who was really a kind-hearted old creature 'come into my warm room and have dinner with me.' The mouse was greatly pleased with Thumbykin, so she said, 'If you like, you can spend the winter with me: of course you will keep my rooms tidy and tell me stories. I am very fond of hearing stories.'

Thumbykin did all the kind old mouse asked her; and in return she was well treated and very comfortable. 'We shall have a visitor soon,' said the field-mouse to Thumbykin one day; 'my neighbour pays me a visit once a week. He is much richer than I am; he has fine large rooms and wears a beautiful black velvet fur. If you could get him for a husband you would indeed be well off. He is blind though, poor man! so you must tell him some of your prettiest stories.' But Thumbykin knew that the neighbour spoken of was only a mole, and she did not mean to trouble herself about him.

The mole however, came and paid his visit. He was dressed in his black velvet coat.

'He is very learned and very rich,' whispered the old field-mouse to Thumbykin, 'and his house is twenty times larger than mine.'

Rich no doubt he was, and learned too; but never having seen the sun or the beautiful flowers, he always spoke slightingly regarding them. Thumbykin found that she had to sing to him; so she sang, 'Lady-bird, lady-bird, fly away home', and 'As I was going along, long, long', and other pretty songs, and the mole at once fell deeply in love with her because she had such a sweet voice; but being a prudent man, he said nothing about his feelings.

A short time before this visit, the mole had dug a long underground passage between the two houses, and he gave the field-mouse and Thumbykin permission to walk in this passage whenever they pleased. But he told them that there was a dead bird lying in the passage, and he begged them not to be frightened by it. 'The bird,' he said, 'was perfect, with beak and feathers all complete. It could not have been dead long, and had been buried just where he had made the passage.' Then the mole took a piece of rotten wood in his mouth, and it shone like fire in the darkness, and he went before them to light them through the long dark passage. When they came to where the dead bird lay the mole pushed his broad nose through the ceiling so as to make a hole.

The daylight fell through the hole and shone on the body of the dead swallow. Its pretty wings were closely folded, and its head and claws were hidden under its feathers. The poor bird had undoubtedly died of cold. It made the little girl very sad to see it, for she dearly loved the little birds. All the summer through they had chirped and sung to please her.

But the unfeeling mole thrust the swallow aside with his crooked legs, and said, 'He will sing no more now. What a wretched thing it must be to be born a bird. Thank Heaven, none of my children will ever be birds. Birds can do nothing but cry Tweet, tweet! and they always starve to death in the winter.'

'Indeed, as a sensible man, you may well say so,' cried the field-mouse. 'What does his chirping and twittering do for a bird when the winter comes? Can his tweet, tweet, appease his hunger, or keep him from being frozen to death? And yet it is thought to be very well bred!' Thumbykin did not speak; but when the other two turned their backs on the dead bird, she stooped down and smoothed aside the feathers that covered the head, and kissed the closed eyelids.

'Perhaps it was you who sang so sweetly to me in the summer,' she said; 'and how much pleasure you gave me, you dear pretty bird!'

The mole then stopped up the hole through which the daylight came, and walked home with the ladies. But at night Thumbykin could not sleep; so she got out of bed, and wove a fine large rug of soft hay. When she had finished it, she gathered together some soft flower down that she found in the field-mouse's sitting-room; and she carried the rug and the down to the dead bird. The down was soft and warm like wool, and she put it carefully round him and spread the coverlet over him, that he might lie warm in the cold earth.

'Good-bye! you dear, pretty little bird,' said she; 'good-bye. Thank you for all the sweet songs you sang in the summer when the trees were green and the sun shone down warmly upon us.' Saying this she laid her head on the breast of the bird, but almost at once she raised it in surprise. It seemed as if something inside the bird was going 'thump, thump'. It was the swallow's heart. The swallow had not been really dead but only numbed with the cold, and when the warmth again stole over him his life came back.

In Autumn all the swallows fly away into warm lands, and if one happens to linger too long, the cold strikes it, and it becomes frozen and falls down as if it were dead, and it lies where it falls and the cold snow covers it.

Thumbykin trembled with fear, for the bird seemed very large in comparison with a little thing like herself, only an inch long. But her pity was stronger than her fear, and being a brave little girl, she covered the poor swallow more thickly with the down, and ran and brought a balsam leaf that she herself had used as a coverlet and spread it over the bird's head.

Next night she again stole into the passage to see him. He was still alive, but he was very weak, and could only open his eyes to look for a moment at his kind little nurse, who stood over him, holding in her hand a rotten piece of wood, for she had no other light.

'Thank you, pretty little maiden,' whispered the sick swallow; 'I am so nice and warm now that I shall soon get back my strength, and be able to fly about again in the warm sunshine.'

'Alas!' said she. 'You must wait for some time. It is too cold out of doors just now, it snows and freezes. You must stay in your warm bed, and I will take care of you.'

Then she brought him some water in a flower-leaf; and when he had drunk it he told her how he had wounded one of his wings in a thorn-bush and was not able to fly as fast as the other swallows; how they flew away without him; and how he fell senseless to the ground. He could not remember any more, and did not know how he came to be where he then lay. All the winter the swallow remained underground, and Thumbykin nursed him with the tenderest care. She did not say a word about the sick swallow to the mole or to the field-mouse, for they did not like birds. Soon the spring came, and the sun warmed the earth, and the swallow said good-bye to his kind little nurse. She opened the hole in the ceiling which the mole had made, and the glorious sunshine poured into the passage, and the swallow begged her to go away with him. 'She could sit on his back,' he said; 'and he would fly away with her into the green woods.' But the little maiden knew that it would vex the old field-mouse if she left her in that way, so she said, 'No, I cannot come.'

'Good-bye then, good-bye, you pretty little darling,' said the swallow; and away he flew into the sunshine. Thumbykin gazed after him and tears filled her eyes. She dearly loved the pretty swallow, whose life she had saved.

'Joy, joy!' sang the bird as he flew away into the green woods. But poor Thumbykin was very sorrowful. She was not able to get out into the warm sunshine; for the corn which the farmer had sown in the field over the house of the field-mouse had grown up so high that it seemed a lofty and pathless wood to the little maiden who was only an inch high.

'Now,' said the field-mouse to her one day, 'you are going to be married, Thumbykin. My neighbour, the mole, has proposed for you. What a piece of luck for a poor girl like you! You must begin at once to get your wedding clothes ready. You must have both woollen and linen, for nothing must be wanting in the wedding outfit of a mole's bride.'

Thumbykin had to set to work with the spindle, and the field-mouse hired four spiders who had to weave day and night. Every evening the mole came to pay his visit, and he always spoke of the time when the summer would be over. Then he said they would be married. Just now the sun was so hot that it burned up the ground and made it as hard as a stone. But the little maiden was not at all happy. She thought the mole tiresome and did not like him. In the morning when the sun rose, and in the evening when he set, she used to creep out at the door, and when the wind blew aside the ears of corn so that she could catch a glimpse of the blue sky, she used to think how lovely it was in the light, and long to see her dear swallow once more. But he never came back again, for by this time he had flown far, far away into the green woods. When the autumn came, Thumbykin had her wedding outfit quite ready; and the field-mouse said to her, 'Well, Thumbykin, in a month now you shall be married.' But the girl cried, and said she would never marry the tiresome mole.

'Nonsense, nonsense!' said the mouse. 'Don't be foolish or I shall bite you with my white teeth. The mole will make you a very handsome husband. The Queen herself does not wear such a handsome black velvet coat. He has, besides, a full kitchen and cellar. You ought to be very thankful for your good fortune.'

At length the wedding-day arrived. The mole came to fetch his bride. Thumbykin would have to go away and live with him deep under the earth, and never again see the warm sun because he did not like it. The poor little maid was very sad at the thought of saying farewell to the beautiful sun: and as the field-mouse had permitted her to stand at the door, she went out to look at it once more, and to say farewell to it.

'Farewell, dear bright sun' she cried, stretching out her arms towards it. Then she walked a little away from the house, for the corn had been cut, and there was only the dry stubble left in the fields. 'Farewell, farewell!' she said again, throwing her arms round a little red flower that grew close beside her. 'Give my love to the swallow, if you should ever see him again.'

Suddenly a 'Tweet, tweet' sounded over her head. She looked up, and there was the swallow himself flying past. As soon as he spied Thumbykin he flew to her with delight, and she told him her story, told him how unwilling she was to marry the stupid mole, and to live always under the earth, and never again see the bright sun. As she told him about her marriage she could not help weeping.

'The cold winter is coming now,' said the swallow, 'and I am going to fly away to a warmer land. Will you come with me? You can sit on my back. Tie yourself on with your girdle. Then we will fly far away from the ugly mole and his gloomy abode; fly far away over the hills to warmer lands—lands where the sunshine is brighter than it is here, where there are lovely flowers, and where it is always summer. Fly away with me now, dear little Thumbykin. You saved my life when I lay frozen in yonder black tunnel.'

'Yes, I will come with you,' said the little maiden. Then she sat down on the bird's back with her feet resting on his outspread wings; and she fastened her girdle to one of his stronger feathers. And the swallow rose high into the air, and flew fast over forest and lake, and over the snow-capped mountains. Poor Thumbykin would have been frozen, but she crept under the bird's warm feathers, peeping out from time to time so that she might catch a glimpse of the beautiful lands over which they were passing. At last they reached the warm countries, where the sun shines much more brightly than it does here, and where the sky seems twice as high above the earth. There by the wayside and on the hedges there grew purple and green and white grapes, and pale lemons and golden oranges hung from the trees in the woods. The air was fragrant with the scent of myrtle and balm, and along the country lanes ran beautiful children, playing with large gay butterflies. The farther the swallow flew the more beautiful every place seemed to grow. At last they came to a lovely blue lake, and by the side of it, shaded by stately green trees, stood a pure white marble castle. It was an old building and, the vine leaves twined round its lofty columns. At the top of these there were many swallows' nests, and one of these was the nest of the swallow who carried Thumbykin.

'This is my house,' said the swallow; 'but it would not do for you to live here. Will you choose for yourself one of those beautiful flowers?—and I will put you down on it, and then you shall have everything you can wish to make you happy.'

'That will be charming,' cried the little maiden; and she clapped her tiny hands.

On the ground lay a large white marble pillar, which had fallen and been broken into three pieces. Between the pieces grew the most beautiful large white flowers. The swallow flew down with Thumbykin and set her on one of the broad leaves. But how surprised she was to see in the middle of the flower, a tiny little man as white and transparent as glass! On his head was a graceful golden crown, and at his shoulders a pair of delicate wings. He was not much larger than the little maid herself. He was the flower-elf. An elf-man and an elf-maid live in every flower, and this was the King of all the flower-elves.

'Oh, how beautiful he is!' whispered Thumbykin to the swallow.

The little flower-king was at first quite frightened at the bird. Compared to such a little thing as himself, it was a giant. But when he saw Thumbykin he was charmed. Never had he seen such a pretty girl. He took the gold crown from his head and placed it on hers; he asked her name, and begged her to marry him, and become as she should the Queen of all the flowers.

This was certainly a very different kind of husband to the son of the toad or to the mole with his black velvet coat; so she said 'yes' to this handsome prince, her new suitor. Then all the flowers opened, and out of each came a tiny lady and gentleman. They were all so graceful that it was a pleasure to look at them. They each brought Thumbykin a present; but the present she loved most of all was a pair of lovely white wings from a big white fly. When these were fastened to her shoulders she could fly from flower to flower.

Then there were great rejoicings, and the little swallow

who sat in his nest overhead was asked to sing for them a wedding song. He sang as well as he could; but his heart was sad, for he was very fond of the little maiden, and had hoped never again to part from her.

'You must no longer be called Thumbykin,' said the flower-elf to her. 'It's an ugly name and you are very beautiful. We will call you Maia.'

'Good-bye, good-bye,' sang the swallow, sad at heart, as he left the warm lands and flew away to the colder North. There he had a nest outside the window of a man who could tell fairy tales. For him the swallow sang 'Tweet, tweet', and that's how we came to hear the whole story.

THE DAISY

In the country, close by the roadside, there stood a manor-house. In front was a little garden full of flowers, surrounded by a painted fence; and on a bank outside the fence there grew, amidst the freshest of grass, a little daisy. The sun shone as brightly and warmly upon the daisy as upon the splendid flowers within the garden, and therefore it grew and grew, till one morning it stood fully open.

She did not fret because she was only a little flower and no one could see her for the grass; she was quite contented. She turned toward the warm sun, looked up to the blue sky, and listened to the lark singing in the air. It did not vex her that she could not do the same. 'I can see and listen,' thought she; 'the sun shines on me, and the wind kisses me. Oh, how richly I am blessed!'

There stood within the palings several grand, stiff-looking flowers; the less scent they had the more airs they gave themselves. The peonies puffed themselves out to make themselves larger than the roses. The tulips had the gayest colours of all; they were perfectly aware of it, and held themselves bolt upright that they might be the better seen. They took no notice at all of the little flowers outside the fence; but she looked at them all the more, thinking, 'How rich and beautiful they are! Yes, that pretty bird will surely fly down and visit them. How happy am I, who live so near them and see their beauty!' Just at that moment the lark did fly down, but he came not to the peonies or the tulips; no, he flew down to the poor little daisy in the grass, who trembled from joy, and knew not what to think, she was so surprised.

The little bird hopped about and sang, 'Oh, how soft is this grass! and what a sweet little flower blooms here, with its golden heart and silver dress!' For the yellow centre of the daisy looked just like gold, and the little petals around gleamed silver white.

How happy the little daisy was no one can ever tell! The bird kissed her with his beak, sang to her, and then flew up again into the warm blue sky. It was a full quarter of an hour before the daisy recovered herself. Half shyly, and yet half in delight, she looked at the flowers in the garden; they must certainly be aware of the honour and happiness that had befallen her, they must know how delighted she was. But the tulips held themselves twice as stiffly as before, and their faces grew quite red with anger. As to the peonies, they were thick-headed and slow, but it was well they could not speak, or the little daisy would have heard something not very pleasant. The poor little flower could see well that they were in an ill-humour, and it made her sad.

Just then, a girl came into the garden with a sharp, bright knife. She went up to the tulips and cut off one after another. 'Oh, that is dreadful!' sighed the daisy; 'it is all over with them now.' Then the girl carried away the tulips.

How glad was the daisy that she grew in the grass outside the palings, and was only a poor little flower! When the sun set, she folded her leaves, went to sleep, and dreamed all night of the sun and the beautiful bird.

The next morning, when our little flower, fresh and cheerful, again spread out all her white leaves to the bright sunshine and clear blue air, she heard the voice of the bird; but he sang mournfully. Alas! the poor lark had good reason for sorrow; he had been caught, and put into a cage close by the open window. He sang of the joys of his free flight, of the young green corn in the fields, and of the pleasure of being borne up by his wings higher and higher. The poor bird was certainly very unhappy; he sat a prisoner in his narrow cage!

The little daisy wished very much to help him; but how could she? And because she could not, she quite forgot how beautiful all around her was, how warmly the sun

shone, and how pretty her own white petals were. Alas!
she could only think of the imprisoned bird.

Just then two little boys came out of the garden. One
of them had a knife in his hand, as large and as sharp as
that with which the girl had cut the tulips. They went up
straight to the little daisy, who could not think what they
wanted.

'Here we can cut a nice piece of turf for the lark,' said
one of the boys; and he began to cut deep all round the
daisy, leaving her in the centre.

'Tear out the flower,' said the other boy. The little
daisy trembled all over for fear; for she knew that if she
were torn out she would die, and she wished so much to
live, as she was to be put into the cage with the lark.

'No, leave it alone,' said the first; 'it looks so pretty!'
So the daisy was left, and was put into the lark's cage.

But the poor bird loudly mourned the loss of its freedom,
and beat its wings against the iron bars of its cage; and
the little flower could not say a single word of comfort to
him, much as she wished to do so. Thus passed the whole
morning.

'There is no water here!' said the lark. 'They have all
gone away and forgotten me. Not a drop of water to
drink! My throat is hot and dry; I feel as if I had fire
and ice within me, and the air is so heavy! Alas! I must
die, I must leave the warm sunshine and the fresh green
fields and all the beautiful things God has made.' Then
he thrust his beak into the cool grass to refresh himself,
and his eye fell on the daisy, and he bowed to her, and said,
'You too will wither here, you poor little flower! They
have given me you, and the little bit of turf around you,
for the whole world outside which I had before! Every
little blade of grass is to be to me a tree and your every
white petal a fragrant flower! Alas! you only make me
think of what I have lost.'

'Oh! that I could comfort him!' thought the daisy.

She could not speak; but the scent from her leaves was
sweeter than it had ever been before, and the lark noticed

it, and though he was fainting with thirst, and in his pain pulled up the blades of grass, he would not touch the daisy.

It was evening, and yet no one came to bring the poor bird a drop of water; he stretched out his pretty wings and fluttered them convulsively; his song died away in a mournful 'Tweet, tweet'; his little head sank beneath the flower, and his heart broke from thirst and grief. The flower could not now, as last night, fold her leaves and sleep; she bent down, sad and sick, to the ground.

The boys did not come till next morning; and when they saw the bird was dead they wept bitterly. They put the bird's dead body into a pretty red box and buried it, and then they strewed the grave with flowers. Like a prince was the poor bird buried! Whilst he lived and sang they forgot him, and left him to die of want in his cage; and now that he was dead his grave was strewn with flowers, and tears were shed over him.

But the turf with the daisy was thrown out into the dusty road. No one thought of the daisy who had felt most for the little bird, and who had so much wished to comfort him.

THE BUCKWHEAT

If after a storm you go through a field in which buckwheat is growing, you will see that it has become quite black, as if it had been burned. I will tell you the why and wherefore as I heard it from the sparrow, who heard it from the lips of an old willow-tree that dwelt near a field of corn and buckwheat, and is there still. The corn was glad to be alive, and grateful too, for the fuller his ears were the lowlier he bent as if in humble thankfulness. The proud buckwheat, however, held his head high and erect.

'I have as many golden ears as the corn,' he said, 'and am far prettier. My flowers are as lovely as apple blossom. Have you ever seen anything more lovely than I am, old willow-tree?'

The willow-tree only nodded, as much as to say, 'That I have.'

'That stupid tree!' said the buckwheat. 'He is so old that the grass is growing out of his body!'

Just then a great storm arose. All the flowers of the field folded their petals, and bent down their little heads. The buckwheat alone stood erect and proud.

'Bend your head as we do,' said the flowers.

'I will not bow,' said the buckwheat.

'Close your flowers and fold your leaves,' said the old willow-tree. 'Do not look up at the lightning, for you will see right into heaven itself. Even men are blinded if they look; what then would happen to us, who are but weeds of the ground, if we dared to do so?'

'Weeds of the ground!' said the buckwheat scornfully; 'I will look up into heaven itself.' The buckwheat in his pride looked upward. For a moment the whole world seemed to be in flames.

When the storm had passed over, how sweet everything

was after the rain! The flowers breathed again, and the corn waved in the wind. But the buckwheat lay on the ground all withered and charred. The old willow-tree shook his head in the wind, and big drops fell from his leaves. It was as if he wept. The sparrows chirped: 'Why do you weep? Do you not breathe the fragrance of flowers and leaves? Why do you weep, old willow-tree?' Then the willow-tree told them what had happened to the proud buckwheat, and I who tell you now heard it all from the sparrows one evening when I asked them for a story.

THE EMPEROR'S NEW CLOTHES

Many years ago there was an Emperor who was so very fond of new clothes that he spent all his money on dress. He did not trouble himself in the least about his soldiers; nor did he care to go either to the theatre or to hunt, except for the occasion they gave him for showing off his new clothes. He had a different suit for each hour of the day; and as of any other king or emperor one is accustomed to say, 'He is sitting in council,' it was always said of him, 'The Emperor is sitting in his wardrobe.'

Time passed merrily in the large town that was his capital. Strangers arrived at the court every day. One day two rogues, calling themselves weavers, made their appearance. They gave out that they knew how to weave stuffs of the most beautiful colours and patterns, but that the clothes made from these had the wonderful property of remaining invisible to every one who was either stupid or unfit for the office he held.

'Those would indeed be splendid clothes!' thought the Emperor. 'Had I such a suit, I might at once find out what men in my realms are unfit for their office, and be able to distinguish the wise from the foolish. This stuff must be woven for me immediately.' And he caused large sums of money to be given to the weavers, that they might begin their work at once.

So the rogues set up two looms, and made a show of working very busily, though in reality they had nothing at all on the looms. They asked for the finest silk and the purest gold thread; put both into their own knapsacks; and then continued their pretended work at the empty looms until late at night.

'I should like to know how the weavers are getting on with my cloth,' thought the Emperor after some time. He was, however, rather nervous when he remembered that a stupid person, or one unfit for his office, would be unable to see the stuff. 'To be sure,' he thought, 'I have nothing to risk in my own person; but yet I would prefer sending somebody else to bring me news about the weavers and their work, before I trouble myself in the affair.' All the city had heard of the wonderful property the cloth was to possess, and all were anxious to learn how worthless and stupid their neighbours were.

'I will send my faithful old minister to the weavers,' concluded the Emperor at last. 'He will be best able to see how the cloth looks; for he is a man of sense, and no one can be better fitted for his post than he is.'

So the faithful old minister went into the hall where the knaves were working with all their might at their empty looms. 'What can be the meaning of this?' thought the old man, opening his eyes very wide. 'I can't see the least bit of thread on the looms!' However, he did not speak aloud.

The rogues begged him most respectfully to be so good as to come nearer; and then asked whether the design pleased him, and whether the colours were not very beautiful, pointing at the same time to the empty frames. The poor old minister looked and looked; he could see nothing on the looms, for there was nothing there. 'What!' thought he, 'is it possible that I am silly? I have never thought so myself; and no one must know it now. Can it be that I am unfit for my office? It will never do for me to say that I could not see the stuff.'

'Well, Sir Minister!' said one of the knaves, still pretending to work, 'you do not say whether the stuff pleases you.'

'Oh, it's very fine!' said the old minister, looking at the loom through his spectacles. 'The pattern and the colours are wonderful. Yes, I will tell the Emperor without delay how very beautiful I think them.'

'We are glad they please you,' said the cheats; and then they named the different colours and described the pattern of the pretended stuff. The old minister paid close attention, that he might repeat to the Emperor what they said. Then the knaves asked for more silk and gold, saying it was needed to complete what they had begun. Of course, they put all that was given them into their knapsacks, and kept on as before working busily at their empty looms.

The Emperor now sent another officer of his court to see how the men were getting on, and to find out whether the cloth would soon be ready. It was just the same with him as with the first. He looked and looked, but could see nothing at all but the empty looms.

'Isn't it fine stuff?' asked the rogues. The minister said he thought it beautiful. Then they began as before, pointing out its beauties and taking of patterns and colours that were not there.

'I certainly am not stupid,' thought the officer. 'It must be that I am not fit for my post. That seems absurd. However, no one shall know it.' So he praised the stuff he could not see, and said he was delighted with both colours and patterns. 'Indeed, your Majesty,' said he to the Emperor when he gave his report, 'the cloth is magnificent.'

The whole city was talking of the splendid cloth that the Emperor was having woven at his own cost.

And now the Emperor thought he would like to see the cloth while it was still on the loom. Accompanied by a select number of officials, among whom were the two honest men who had already admired the cloth, he went to the cunning weavers who, when aware of the Emperor's approach, went on working more busily than ever, although they did not pass a single thread through the looms.

'Is it not absolutely magnificent?' said the two officers who had been there before. 'If your Majesty will only be pleased to look at it! what a splendid design! what glorious colours!' And at the same time they pointed to the empty looms; for they thought that every one else could see the cloth.

'How is this?' said the Emperor to himself; 'I can see nothing! Oh, this is dreadful! Am I a fool? Am I

unfit to be an Emperor? That would be the worst thing
that could happen to me.—Oh! the cloth is charming,'
said he aloud. 'It has my complete approval.' And he
smiled most graciously, and looked closely at the empty
looms; for on no account would he say that he could not
see what two of the officers of his court had praised so
much. All the retinue now looked and looked, but they
could see nothing any more than the others. Neverthe-
less, they all exclaimed, 'Oh, how beautiful!' and advised
His Majesty to have some new clothes made from this
splendid material for the approaching procession. 'Magnificent! charming! excellent!' resounded on all sides; and
every one seemed greatly pleased. The Emperor showed
his satisfaction by making the rogues knights, and giving
them the title of 'Gentlemen Weavers to the Emperor'.

The two rogues sat up the whole of the night before the
day of the procession. They had sixteen candles burning,
so that every one might see how hard they were working to
finish the Emperor's new suit. They pretended to roll the
cloth off the looms; they cut the air with great scissors,
and sewed with needles without any thread in them.
'See!' cried they at last; 'the Emperor's new clothes are
ready!'

And now the Emperor, with all the grandees of his court,
came to the weavers. The rogues raised their arms, as if
holding something up, and said, 'Here are your Majesty's
trousers! here is the scarf! here is the mantle! The whole
suit is as light as a cobweb. You might fancy you had on
nothing at all when dressed in it; that, however, is the
great virtue of this fine cloth.'

'Yes, indeed!' said all the courtiers, although not one
of them could see anything; because there was nothing to
be seen.

'If your Imperial Majesty will be graciously pleased to
take off your clothes, we will fit on the new suit in front
of the large looking-glass,' said the swindlers.

The Emperor accordingly took off his clothes, and the
rogues pretended to put on him separately each article of

his new suit, the Emperor turning round from side to side before the looking-glass.

'How splendid His Majesty looks in his new clothes! and how well they fit!' every one cried out. 'What a design! what colours! These are indeed royal robes!'

'The attendants are waiting outside with the canopy which is to be borne over your Majesty in the procession,' announced the chief master of the ceremonies.

'I am quite ready,' answered the Emperor. 'Do my new clothes fit well?' he asked, turning himself round again before the looking-glass as if he was carefully examining his handsome suit.

The lords of the bedchamber, who were to carry His Majesty's train, felt about on the ground, as if they were lifting up the ends of the mantle, and walked as if they were holding up a train; for they feared to show that they saw nothing and so be thought stupid for their office.

So in the midst of the procession the Emperor walked under his high canopy through the streets of his capital. And all the people standing by, and those at the windows, cried out, 'Oh! how beautiful are our Emperor's new clothes! what a train there is to the mantle! and how gracefully the scarf hangs!' In short, no one would allow that he could not see those much-admired clothes; because, in doing so, he would have declared himself either a fool or unfit for his office. Certainly, none of the Emperor's previous suits had made such an impression as this.

'But the Emperor has nothing on at all!' said a little child.

'Listen to the voice of innocence!' exclaimed her father; and what the child had said was whispered from one to another.

'But he has on nothing at all!' at last cried out all the people. The Emperor was vexed, for he felt that the people were right; but he thought the procession must go on now. And the lords of the bedchamber took greater pains than ever to appear holding up a train, although, in reality, there was no train to hold.

*The Emperor walked under his high canopy through
the streets of his capital*

THE REAL PRINCESS

There was once a Prince who wished to marry a Princess; but then she must be a real Princess. He travelled all over the world in hopes of finding such a one; but there was always something wrong. Princesses he found in plenty; but he could not make up his mind that they were real Princesses, for now one thing, now another, seemed to him not quite right about them. At last he went back to his palace quite downcast, because he wished so much to have a real Princess for his wife, and he had not been able to find one.

One evening a fearful tempest arose. It thundered and lightened, and the rain came down in torrents. Besides, it was dark as pitch. All at once there was a violent knocking at the door, and the old King, the Prince's father, went out himself to open it.

It was a Princess who was standing outside. What with the rain and the wind, she was in a sad state; the water trickled from her hair, and her clothes clung to her body. She said she was a real Princess.

'Ah, we shall soon see about that!' thought the old Queen-mother. She gave no hint whatever of what she was going to do, but went quietly into the bedroom, took all the bed-clothes off the bed, and put three little peas on the bedstead. Then she laid twenty mattresses one upon another over the three peas, and put twenty feather-beds over the mattresses.

Upon this bed the Princess was to pass the night.

The next morning she was asked how she had slept. 'Oh, very badly indeed!' she replied. 'I have scarcely closed my eyes the whole night through. I do not know what was in my bed, but I had something hard under me, and am all over black and blue. It has hurt me so much!'

Now it was plain that this must be a real Princess, since she had been able to feel the three little peas through the twenty mattresses and twenty feather-beds. None but a real Princess could have had such a delicate sense of feeling.

So the Prince made her his wife, being now convinced that he had found a real Princess. The three peas were, however, put into the royal museum, where they are still to be seen, if they have not been stolen.

Notice that this is a true story.

THE GARDEN OF PARADISE

There was once a young Prince who had so many and such beautiful books, that he could find in them anything he wished to know except where the Garden of Paradise was to be found, and this was just what he wished most to know.

When he was a very little boy, just beginning to go to school, his grandmother told him that every flower in the Garden of Paradise tasted like the sweetest of cakes, and that the stamens were full of the choicest wines. On one flower there grew history, on another geography, on a third tables; so that whoever ate the flower immediately knew his lesson; the more he ate, the more he learned of history, geography, or arithmetic.

At that time the young Prince believed it all; but when he grew bigger and wiser, and learned more, he saw plainly that the beauty of the Garden of Paradise must be something quite different. 'Oh, why did Eve pluck the fruit of the tree of knowledge of good and evil? and why did Adam eat of the forbidden fruit?' he kept thinking. 'Had I been there it would not have happened, and so there would have been no sin in the world.' Until he was seventeen years old, he kept constantly thinking about the Garden of Paradise.

One day he went into the wood; he went alone; for to wander thus was his chief delight.

The evening drew on, the clouds gathered, and the rain poured down as if the sky were nothing but a vast waterspout. It was as dark as it is at midnight in the deepest of wells. The Prince now slipped on the wet grass, now stumbled over the bare rocks that projected from the stony ground. Everything was dripping with water, and the poor Prince had not a dry thread on him. His strength was failing when he heard a strange rushing noise, and saw before him a large lighted cavern. In the middle of the cave a huge fire was burning, and a fine stag was being roasted before it. A woman, elderly but tall and strong, as if she were a man in disguise, sat by the fire, throwing upon it one piece of wood after another. 'Come in,' she said to the Prince; 'sit down by the fire and dry your clothes.'

'There is a great draught here,' said the Prince, as he sat down on the ground.

'It will be still worse when my sons come home,' answered the woman. 'You are now in the Cavern of the Winds; my sons are the Four Winds. Do you understand?'

'Where are your sons?' asked the Prince.

'There is no use in answering stupid questions,' said the woman. 'My sons have plenty of work on hand; they are playing at ball with the clouds up there in the King's hall!' and she pointed upwards.

'Indeed!' said the Prince. 'You speak more harshly, and are not so gentle as the woman I am used to.'

'Yes, they have nothing else to do! I must be harsh if I am to keep my boys in order; and I can do it, though they are very headstrong. Do you see those four sacks hanging by the wall? They are as much afraid of them as you used to be of the switch behind the looking-glass. I bend them together, and then they must get into the sacks. They know they must obey, I can tell you. There they sit, and dare not try to come out till it pleases me. But here comes one of them!'

It was the North Wind. He brought icy coldness with him; large hailstones rattled on the floor, and flakes of snow flew all round him. He wore a jacket and trousers of bear's skin, a cap of seal's skin was drawn down over his ears; long icicles hung from his beard, and one hailstone after another fell from under the collar of his jacket.

'Don't go too near the fire,' said the Prince; 'you may get your face and hands frost-bitten.'

'Frost-bitten!' laughed the North Wind. 'Frost is my greatest delight! But what spindle-shanked boy are you, and how did you get into the Cavern of the Winds?'

'He is my guest,' said the old woman; 'and if you are not content with that explanation, you may go into the sack! Now, you know.'

This was quite enough. The North Wind began to tell whence he came, and how he had spent the last month.

'I come from the Polar Seas,' said he. 'I have been on the Bear's Island, along with the Russian whalers. I sat and slept at the helm of their ship when they sailed from the North Cape. Whenever I woke up I found the stormy petrels flying about my feet. They are strange birds. They give one flap with their wings and then hold them stretched out straight and fly away.'

'Don't make such a story of it,' said his mother. 'Come to the point; what sort of place is Bear's Island?'

'That is a glorious place!' said the North Wind. 'The ground seems made for dancing on, it is smooth and flat as a plate. Half-melted snow partly covered with moss, sharp stones, and the skeletons of whales and polar bears are strewed over it, looking like the arms and legs of giants, covered with musty green. You would fancy the sun had never shone there. I blew gently to clear away the clouds, and there I saw a little shed, built from the wood of a wreck, and covered with walrus skins with the fleshy side out. A living polar bear sat growling on the roof. I walked on the shore, peeped into birds' nests, looked at the poor naked young ones, who were crying with their beaks wide open; I blew into their little throats, and they learned to be quiet. Farther on the walruses with their swine-like heads, and teeth an ell long, rolled like gigantic worms beneath the waters.

'And now the fishery began; the harpoon was thrust into the breast of the sea-horse, and the blood spirted up like a fountain and streamed over the ice. Then I thought of my part of the sport. I began to blow, and set my ships, the icebergs, sailing to crush the boats. Oh! how the sailors screamed and shouted; but I screamed still louder. They were forced to unload their cargo, and to throw the dead walruses, and their chests, and the ship's cordage, out upon the ice. I shook snow-flakes over them, and left them in their crushed boats to drift southwards to taste sea-water. They will never come again to Bear's Island!'

'Then you have done mischief!' said the mother of the Winds.

'What good I have done, others may tell,' said he. 'But here comes my brother of the West. I love him the best of all: he smells of the sea, and has a right healthy coldness about him.'

'Can that be little Zephyr?' asked the Prince.

'Yes, it is Zephyr,' said the old woman; 'but little he is no longer. In days of yore he was a pretty boy; but those times have long passed away.'

He came in looking like a wild man, but he had on a sort of padded hat, that his head might not be hurt. In his hand he held a club of mahogany cut in the American forests, no trifling thing to carry.

'Whence come you?' asked the mother.

'From those forest wastes,' said he, 'where the thorny brambles weave hedges between the trees, where the water snake sleeps in the damp grass, and men seem to be unknown.'

'What did you there?'

'I looked at the deep river, marked how it hurled itself from the rocks, and flew like dust towards the clouds, that it might give birth to the rainbow. I saw a buffalo swimming in the river; but the strong stream carried him down. A flock of wild geese were swimming there too. They flew up into the air when they neared the waterfall, leaving the buffalo to be hurled over it. That pleased me, so I raised such a storm as uprooted old trees and brought them to the ground with a crash, broken to splinters, or sent them careering down the stream.'

'And have you done nothing else?' said the old woman.

'I have rushed wildly across the Savannahs; I have stroked wild horses, and shaken the cocoa-nut trees. Yes, yes, I have many stories to tell! But we need not tell all we know. That you know well, don't you, old lady?' And he kissed his mother so roughly that she almost fell. He was a wild fellow.

Now came the South Wind in his turban and floating Bedouin mantle.

'It is very cold here,' said he, as he threw wood upon the fire. 'It is easy to see that the North Wind has arrived before me.'

'Why, it's hot enough to roast a bear,' said the North Wind.

'You're a bear yourself,' said the South Wind.

'Do you wish, both of you, to go into the sack?' asked the old woman. 'Sit down on that stone there and tell me where you have been.'

'In Africa, mother,' answered he. 'I have been hunting lions in the land of the Kaffirs. Such beautiful grass grows on those plains, green as olives! There the ostrich ran races with me, but I was yet swifter than he. I came to the yellow sands of the desert. There one might fancy oneself at the bottom of the sea. I met with a caravan; they had just killed their last camel, in hopes of getting water to drink, but they did not find much. The sun was burning over their heads, the sands roasting beneath their feet. There seemed no end to the desert. I rolled myself up in the fine loose sand, and threw it up into the form of an immense pillar; a famous dance it had! You should have seen how frightened the dromedaries looked, and how the merchants drew their caftans over their heads. They threw themselves down before me as they are wont to do before Allah. There they are all buried. A pyramid of sand stands over them. If I should one day blow it away, the sun will bleach their bones; and travellers will see that people have been there before them; otherwise, in such a desert, they might think it impossible.'

'Then you have only done evil!' said the mother. 'March into the sack!' And before he was aware of it, the South Wind was seized and popped into the sack, which rolled about on the floor until the mother sat down on it to keep it still.

These boys of yours are desperately wild,' said the Prince.

'Yes, indeed,' answered she; 'but I know how to make them obey. Here is the fourth.'

Then in came the East Wind, dressed like a Chinaman.

'Oh! you come from the quarter, do you!' said the mother. 'I thought you had been to the Garden of Paradise.'

'I shall go there tomorrow,' said the East Wind. 'I have not been there for a hundred years. I now come from China, where I danced round the porcelain tower, till all the bells began to ring. In the street below there was an official flogging going on, and bamboos were being broken on the shoulders of people, from the first to the ninth rank, who cried out, "Thanks, thanks, my fatherly benefactor!" But the words came not from their hearts; so I rang the bells till they sounded, "Ding, ding, dong!"'

'You are a wild boy,' said the mother. 'It is well that you go tomorrow to the Garden of Paradise. Your visits there always improve you. Remember to drink deeply there from the fountain of wisdom, and bring me home a flaskful.'

'I will do so,' said the East Wind. 'But why have you put brother South into the sack? Let him come out. I want him to tell me all about the bird called the phœnix. The Princess, when I visit her once in a hundred years, always asks me about that bird. Open the sack, mother! and I will give you two cupfuls of tea, as fresh and green as when I plucked it.'

'Well, then, for the sake of the tea, and because you are my darling, I will open the sack.' She did so, and the South Wind crept out; but he looked quite ashamed because the stranger Prince had seen his disgrace.

'Here is a palm leaf for the Princess,' said the South Wind; 'it was given to me by the old phœnix, the only one in the world. He has scrawled on it, with his beak, his whole history during the hundred years of his life. The Princess can read for herself how the phœnix set fire to his own nest; and sat therein and was burned like a Hindoo widow. How the dry branches crackled! How the smoke and steam rose from the burning nest! At last everything was consumed by the flames, the old phœnix was in ashes; but his egg lay glowing in the fire, it burst with a loud noise, and the young one flew out. He is now king over all the birds, and the only phœnix in the world. He has bitten a hole in the leaf I gave you; that is his greeting to the Princess.'

'Well, now, let us have something to eat,' said the mother of the Winds; and accordingly they all sat down to partake of the roasted stag. The Prince sat next to the East Wind, and they soon became good friends.

'What Princess is that of whom you have been talking?' said the Prince, 'and where is the Garden of Paradise?'

'Ha, ha!' said the East Wind, 'do you wish to go there? Well, then, fly with me tomorrow; but I must tell you that no human being has been there since Adam and Eve's time. You have read of them in your Bible, I suppose?'

'Of course I have,' answered the Prince.

'Well, when they were driven out of it, the Garden sank under the earth; but it still kept its warm sunshine, its balmy air, and all its beauty. The queen of the fairies makes it her abode, and there also is the Island of Bliss, where death never comes, and where life is so beautiful! I can take you there tomorrow if you seat yourself on my back. But don't talk any more now, for I wish to sleep.' And then they all went to sleep.

When the Prince awoke in the morning, he was not a little astonished to find himself already far above the clouds. He was sitting on the back of the East Wind, who kept tight hold of him; and they flew so high that woods and meadows, rivers and seas, appeared like a large coloured map.

'Good-morning!' said the East Wind. 'You may as well sleep a little longer, for there is not much to be seen in the flat country beneath us, unless you like to count the churches; they stand like little bits of chalk on the green board there below.' By the green board he meant the fields and meadows.

'It was rude of me not to say good-bye to your mother and brothers,' said the Prince.

'They'll excuse you as you were asleep,' said the East Wind. And now they flew on faster than ever. How fast, might be seen by the rustling of the trees as they passed them; by the waves rising higher on the seas and lakes as they crossed them; and by the large ships dipping down into the water like swans diving.

In the evening, when it became dark, the large towns had a most curious appearance. Lights were burning here and there; it was just like watching the sparks on a burnt piece of paper as they go out one after the other. The Prince clapped his hands; but the East Wind begged him to be quiet and to hold fast, as otherwise he might fall, and be left hanging from the top of a church steeple.

'Now you can see the Himalaya mountains,' said the East Wind; 'they are the highest in Asia. We shall soon come now to the Garden of Paradise.' So they turned more towards the South, and soon inhaled the fragrance of spices and flowers. Figs and pomegranates were growing wild; blue and purple grapes hung from the vines. Here they descended and stretched themselves on the soft grass, while the flowers nodded to the Wind, as if they wished to say, 'Welcome, welcome!'

'Are we now in the Garden of Paradise?' asked the Prince.

'No, not yet,' said the East Wind, 'but we shall soon be there. Do you see yon rock, and the cavern beneath it, in front of which the vine branches hang like a large green curtain? We must go through that. Wrap your cloak about you; for though the sun scorches here, a step farther on and you will find it as cold as ice. The bird that is flying past the cave has one wing warm as summer, and the other as cold as winter.'

'This, then, is the way to the Garden of Paradise!' said

the Prince as they went into the cave. It was bitter cold;
but the cold did not last long, for the East Wind spread out
his wings and they shone like the purest flame. What a
cavern it was! Large blocks of stone, from which water
was trickling, hung in the strangest shapes above them.
Sometimes it was so narrow that they had to creep along on
their hands and knees, and at other times it was so lofty and
wide, they might have been in the open air. It looked like
a chapel for the dead with its silent organ turned to stone.

'Surely we are going through the Valley of Death, to
reach the Garden of Paradise?' said the Prince; but the
East Wind pointed without a word to where the loveliest
blue light was beaming to meet them. The rocks above
them grew like mists, and at last were as clear and bright
as white clouds in the moonlight. The air was balmy, fresh
as a breeze among the mountains, and fragrants as one blowing through a valley of roses. A river, as clear as the air
itself, flowed at their feet. Gold and silver fish swam in it;
purple eels, that emitted blue sparks at every motion, were
playing beneath its surface, and the broad leaves of the
water-lilies that floated upon it shone with all the colours
of the rainbow. The glowing orange-coloured flower itself
seemed to draw its nourishment from the water, as the flame
of a lamp draws its nourishment from the oil. A bridge
of marble, of such cunning workmanship that it seemed
made of lace and pearl, lead over the water to the Island of
Bliss, where bloomed the Garden of Paradise. The East
Wind carried the Prince over. The flowers and leaves
sang the sweetest songs about his childhood, in tones so soft
and full that no human voice could match them. Whether
they were palm-trees of gigantic water-plants that grew here
the Prince knew not; but he had never before seen trees so
large and full of sap; and hanging about them in long
wreaths like the illuminations on the margins of old missals
were the most singular creepers. Birds, flowers, and scrolls
were mingled in the strangest confusion. Close to them, in
the grass, stood a flock of peacocks, with their bright tails
spread out. The Prince touched them, but found to his

surprise that they were not birds but plants: they were plantain-leaves, that sparkled like the tails of peacocks. Lions and tigers, perfectly tame, sprang like cats over green hedges, from which there came a scent like that of the sweet-smelling flower of the olive. The timid wood-turtle, her plumage bright as the loveliest pearl, flapped her wings against the lion's mane; and the shy antelope stood by, and nodded his head as if he too wished to play.

And now came the Fairy of Paradise. Her garments shone like the sun, and her face, like that of a happy mother rejoicing over her child, beamed with delight. She was young and beautiful, and a train of lovely maidens followed her, each having a star sparkling in her hair. The East Wind gave her the leaf of the phœnix, and her eyes beamed with joy. She took the Prince by the hand, and led him into her palace, the walls of which were coloured like a tulip-leaf when it is held towards the sun. The roof was like a flower turned upside down, whose cup appeared the deeper the longer you looked into it. The Prince stepped to the window, and looked through one of the panes, and there he saw what seemed to be the tree of knowledge of good and evil, with the Serpent, and Adam and Eve, standing beside it. 'Were they not driven out?' asked he. The Fairy smiled, and told him that Time had marked each event on a window pane in the form of a picture; but that these were not like common pictures, for everything in them lived; the leaves of the trees moved, and men came and went, as in a mirror. He looked through another pane, and there saw Jacob's dream; the ladder rose to Heaven, and angels with their large wings were moving up and down. Yes, everything that had happened in the world lived and moved in the panes of glass. Time only could have made such cunning pictures.

The Fairy now led the Prince into a spacious hall, whose walls seemed transparent and were covered with portraits, each more lovely than another. There were millions of blessed spirits, whose laughter and song made one sweet melody. In the midst of the hall stood a large tree with drooping branches. Golden apples, of different sizes, hung like oranges among the green leaves. This was the tree of knowledge of good and evil, of the fruit of which Adam and Eve did eat. From every leaf there dropped a bright red drop of dew, as though the tree wept tears of blood for our first parents' sin.

'Let us get into the boat,' said the Fairy; 'we shall find it refreshing. The boat is rocked on the swelling waves, without stirring from its place; and all the countries in the world appear to glide past.' And it was indeed strange to see. First came the high, snow-covered Alps, with their clouds and dark fir-trees. The horn's deep tones were heard, as was the voice of the herdsman singing merrily in the valley below. Then the banyan-trees bent their long drooping branches over the boat, coal-black swans glided over the water, and the strangest-looking animals and flowers were to be seen on the distant shore. It was Australia, the fifth division of the world, that now glided by with the blue mountains in the background. And now came the hymns of priests, the dance of savages, accompanied by the noise of drums and the clang of bone trumpets. Egypt's cloud-aspiring pyramids, overthrown pillars, and sphinxes sailed by. The northern lights flashed over the extinct volcanoes of the North, in fireworks such as no mortal could imitate. The Prince was so happy! He saw a hundred times more than we have related here.

'And may I stay here always?' asked he.

'That depends upon yourself,' answered the Fairy. 'If you do not, like Adam, do what is forbidden, you may stay here always.'

'I will not touch the fruit of the tree of knowledge of good and evil,' said the Prince; 'there are a thousand fruits here quite as beautiful!'

'Examine your own heart,' said the Princess, 'and if you do not feel strong enough, return with the East Wind who brought you. He is just going to fly back, and he will not return for a hundred years. The time will pass away here as if it were only a hundred hours; but it is a long time for temptation and sin. Every evening when I leave you, I must invite you to "Come with me!" I must beckon to you, but—beware of attending to my call. Come not with me, for every step will but increase the temptation. You will come into the hall where the tree of knowledge of good and evil stands; I shall sleep among its fragrant hanging branches; you will bend over me, and if you touch me, Paradise will sink beneath the earth, and be lost to you. The sharp wind of the desert will whistle around, the cold rain will drip from your hair, sorrow and care will be your lot.'

'I will stay here,' said the Prince. And the East Wind kissed his forehead, and said: 'Be strong, and we shall see each other again after a hundred years. Farewell, farewell!' Then he spread out his great wings which shone like lightning in harvest-time, or the northern lights in winter. 'Farewell, farewell!' resounded from the trees and flowers. Storks and pelicans, like a long streaming ribbon, flew after him, accompanying him to the end of the garden.

'Now we will begin our dances,' said the Fairy, 'and when the sun is sinking, while I am dancing with you, you will see me beckon, you will hear me say, "Come with me". But do not follow. For a hundred years I must repeat this call to you every evening. Every day, if you resist, your strength will increase, till at last you will not even think of following. This evening will be the first time,—I have warned you!'

The Fairy then led him into a large hall, filled with white transparent lilies, whose yellow stamens formed little golden harps, sending forth clear, sweet tones resembling those of the flute.

The sun was setting; the whole sky was like pure gold; and the lilies shone amid the purple gleam, like the loveliest roses. The Prince saw the background of the hall opening, and there stood the tree of knowledge of good and evil in a splendour that dazzled his eyes. A song floated over him, sweet and gentle as his mother's voice. It seemed as though she said, 'My child; my dear, dear child!'

Then the Fairy beckoned gracefully, saying, 'Come with me, come with me!' and he rushed to her, forgetting his promise, even on this the first evening.

The fragrance, the spicy fragrance around, grew stronger; the harps sounded more sweetly; and it seemed as though the millions of smiling heads, in the hall where the tree of knowledge of good and evil was growing, nodded and sang, 'Let us know everything! Man is lord of the earth!' And they were no longer tears of blood that dropped from the leaves of the tree of knowledge of good and evil; they were red sparkling stars—so it appeared to him.

'Come with me, come with me!' Thus spoke those trembling tones; and the Fairy bent the boughs asunder, and in another moment was hidden within them.

'I have not yet sinned,' said the Prince, 'neither will I.' He flung aside the boughs where she was sleeping— beautiful as only the Fairy of the Garden of Paradise could be. She smiled as she slept. He bent over her, and saw tears tremble behind her eyelashes. 'Weepest thou for me?' whispered he. 'Weep not, loveliest of beings!' Then he kissed the tears from her eyes; he kissed her lips. There was a fearful clap of thunder, more loud and deep than any that had ever been heard. All things rushed together in wild confusion; the charming Fairy vanished; the blooming Paradise sank so low! so low! The Prince saw it sink amid the darkness of night; it shone in the distance like a little glimmering star. A deadly coldness shot through his limbs; his eyes closed and he lay for some time apparently dead.

The cold rain was beating upon his face; the sharp wind was blowing upon his forehead, when the Prince's consciousness returned.

'What have I done?' said he. 'I have sinned like Adam; I have sinned, and Paradise has sunk low, beneath the earth!' And he opened his eyes and saw the star in the distance, the star which sparkled like his lost Paradise. It was the morning star.

He stood upright, and found himself in the wood, near the Cavern of the Winds. The mother of the Winds sat by his side; she looked very angry, and raised her hand. 'Already, on the first evening!' said she. 'Truly I expected it. Well, if you were my son, you should go forthwith into the sack.'

'He shall go there!' said Death. He was a strong old man, with a scythe in his hand, and with large black wings. 'He shall be laid in the coffin, but not yet. I shall suffer him to wander a little while upon the earth to repent of his sin. He may improve, he may grow good. I shall return one day when he least expects it and lay him in the black coffin. If his head and heart are still full of sin, he will sink lower than the Garden of Paradise sank; but if he have become good and holy, I shall put the coffin on my head, and fly to the star yonder. The Garden of Paradise blooms there also; and he shall enter and remain in the star, that bright sparkling star, for ever!'

ELDER-TREE MOTHER

There was once a little boy who had caught a cold by getting his feet wet; how he did it no one could think, for the weather was perfectly fine and dry. His mother took off his clothes, put him to bed, and brought in the tea-pot, to make him a cup of good, warm elder-tea. Just then the kind old man, who lodged in the uppermost floor of the house, came in. He lived quite alone, poor man! for he had neither wife nor children of his own; but he loved children very much, and had so many charming stories and fairy tales to tell them that it was a pleasure to see him among them.

'Now drink your tea, like a good boy,' said the mother, 'and who knows but you may hear a story.'

'Ah, yes, if one could only think of something new!' said the old man, smiling and nodding. 'But how did the little one get his feet wet?'

'How, indeed?' said the mother. 'That's just what nobody can make out.'

'May not I have a story?' asked the boy.

'Yes,' answered the old man; 'if you can tell me exactly how deep the gutter is in the little street yonder, along which you go to school. I want to know that first.'

'The water just comes half-way up to my knee,' replied the boy, 'but not unless I walk through the deep hole.'

'Ah, then, that's where we got our wet feet!' said the old man. 'And now, I suppose I shall tell you a story, but really I don't know any more.'

'But you can make up one in a moment,' said the boy. 'Mother says that everything you look at quickly becomes a fairy tale, and that everything you touch you turn into a story.'

'Yes, but those stories and fairy tales are not good for much! The right sort comes of their own accord; they tap at my forehead, and cry, "Here we are!"'

'Will they not come and tap soon?' said the little boy; and his mother laughed, put some elder-flowers into the tea-pot, and poured boiling water over them.

'Tell me a story, do!' said the little boy.

'Yes, if a story would come of itself; but they are proud, and only come when they please. Hush!' cried he all of a sudden, 'here we have it! Look out; now it is in the tea-pot!'

The little boy looked at the tea-pot. He saw the lid rise higher and higher, and elder-flowers spring forth as fresh and white as snow, and long branches sprouted from the spout, spreading on all sides, and growing larger and larger, till at last there stood by the bedside a most charming elder-bush, a perfect tree, some of its boughs stretching over the bed and thrusting the curtains aside. Oh, how it blossomed and how sweet it smelled! And in the midst of the tree sat a kind-looking old dame, wearing a wonderful dress. It was green like the elder-leaves, and had large white elder-flower clusters spreading all over it. One could not be sure whether it were made of some woven stuff or of real, living green leaves and flowers.

'What is her name?' asked the little boy.

'Why, those old Greeks and Romans used to call her Dryad,' answered the old man, 'but we don't understand those outlandish names. The sailors have a much better name for her; they call her Little Elder-Tree Mother, and that suits her very well. Now, you must attend to her. Listen, and keep looking at the pretty elder-tree.

'Just such another large, blooming tree as this stands outside in the corner of a poor little yard. Under this tree there sat, one bright, sunny afternoon, two old people—a very, very old sailor, and his very, very old wife. They were great-grandparents already, and would soon have to keep their golden wedding, but they could not exactly remember on what day it would fall. Elder-Tree Mother sat in the tree above them, looking as pleased as she does now. 'Ah, I know when the golden wedding-day is!' said she; but they did not hear her, they were talking over old times.

'"Do you remember?" said the sailor, "when we were quite little, and used to be always running and playing about in this very yard where we are now sitting, and how we stuck slips in the ground to make a garden?"

'"To be sure I remember!" replied the old woman. "We watered the slips every day, and one of them was an elder-slip and took root, and it put out its green shoots till it grew up to be this large tree that we old folks are now sitting under."

'"So it did!" said the sailor; "and in the corner yonder used to stand the water-butt, where I sailed my boats. I cut them out with my own hand. Such splendid boats they were! To be sure, I have seen a different kind of sailing since then."

'"Yes, but first we went to school," said his wife. "And then we were confirmed; we both of us cried, I remember. And in the afternoon of that day we went hand in hand up to the Round Tower, and saw the view round Copenhagen and across the sea; and then we went to Fredericksberg, where the King and Queen were sailing about in their beautiful boat."

'"But I had to go away, and sail in very different parts," said the old sailor, "and for many, many years I was away on those long voyages!"

'"Yes, and how often I wept for you!" said she. "I thought you must be dead and lying drowned at the bottom of the sea. Many a night I got up to look at the weather-cock, to see if the wind had turned; and turn it did, over and over again, but you came not back. There is one day I shall never forget. It was pouring with rain. The dust-men had come to the house where I was in service. I went down with the dust-box and stood for a little near the dust-bin; and while I stood the postman came up and gave me a letter. It was from you. I tore it open and read it. I laughed and cried by turns, I was so happy. The letter told me you were in the warm countries, where the coffee-trees grow. What charming countries those must be! It told me so many things; and there I stood at the door of the dust-bin reading it, while the rain kept pouring down in torrents. Just then somebody came up behind me, and took hold of me——"

"'Yes, indeed, and didn't you give him a good box on the ear! Didn't his ear tingle after it!"

"'But I did not know that it was you. You had arrived as soon as your letter; and you were so handsome!—but that you are still,—and you had a large yellow silk handkerchief in your pocket and a new hat on your head. Oh, what weather it was! the streets were quite flooded."

"'And then we were married," said the sailor; "don't you remember that? And then we had our first little boy, and after him came Marie, and Niels, and Peter, and Hans Christian."

"'Yes," said she, "all grown up now, and all respectable men and women, whom every one likes."

"'And now their children too, they have little ones," added the old sailor. "Yes, they are fine healthy babies, those great-grandchildren of ours! I fancy it was just about this time of year that we were married."

"'Yes, today is your golden wedding-day!" said Elder-Tree Mother, bending down her head to the old people; but they thought it was a neighbour speaking, and they gave little heed, but looked at each other, and clasped each other's hand. Presently the children and grandchildren, who knew that this was the golden wedding-day, came. They had come that very morning to congratulate their parents, but the old people had quite forgotten that, although they could remember so clearly things that had happened half a century before. And the elder-blossoms smelled so sweetly, and the sun, which was near setting, shed such a rosy light on the old couple's faces; while the youngest of the grandchildren danced round them, shouting with glee that they were all to have a feast to-night, and hot potatoes for supper. And Elder-Tree Mother nodded her head to them from the tree, and shouted "Hurrah!" with the others.'

'But that's not a fairy tale,' said the little boy who had been listening to the story.

'Not till you understand it,' said the old story-teller. 'Let us ask Elder-Tree Mother to explain it.'

'No! That was not a fairy tale,' said Elder-Tree Mother; 'but now you shall have one, and a true one too. The most charming fairy tales spring out of the common events of everyday life just as my pretty elder-bush has grown out of the tea-pot!' And then she took the little boy out of bed, pillowing his head upon her bosom, and the elder-boughs so richly laden with blossoms twined around them, so that they seemed to be sitting in a thick-leaved fragrant arbour. And the arbour flew away with them through the air in the most delightful way. Elder-Tree Mother had, all at once, changed into a pretty and graceful young girl. Her dress was the same as Elder-Tree Mother had worn; but on her bosom rested a real elder-flower cluster. Her eyes were large and blue, and charming to behold, and a garland of elder-flowers was wreathed among her curling flaxen hair. She and the boy kissed each other, and immediately they were of the same age, and were very happy.

Hand in hand they walked out of the arbour, and found themselves in the pretty flower-garden of their home. On the lawn they found their father's walking-stick tied up. For the children there was life in the stick. As soon as they got astride it, the bright knob became a fiery, neighing head, a long black mane fluttered to and fro in the wind, and four strong slender legs shot out. Their new steed was a spirited creature, and galloped with them round the grass plot. 'Hurrah! Now we will ride many miles away,' said the boy; 'let us ride to the dear old manor house we went to last year.' Round and round the lawn they rode, and the little girl, who, as we know, was no other than Elder-Tree Mother, kept crying out all the while, 'Now we are in the country. See yon pretty cottage! The elder-tree is spreading its branches over it, and the cock is marching about and scratching for the hens. See how he struts! Now we are close to the church. It stands high on the hill, amongst the great oak-trees. Now we are at the smithy; the fire is blazing, and the half-clad men are banging away with their hammers, and the sparks are flying about. Away, away, to the old manor house!' And all that the little maid spoke of flew past them. The boy saw it all, and still they only rode round and round the lawn. Then they played in one of the walks, and raked up the ground to make out a tiny garden for themselves; and the girl took one of the elder-blossoms out of her hair, and planted it, and it grew up, just as the elder-spri ggrew which was planted by the old sailor and his wife when they were little ones. Then the little girl threw her arms round the little boy's waist, and away they flew over all the country. Spring deepened into summer, and summer mellowed into autumn, and autumn faded into pale, cold winter, and a thousand pictures were mirrored in the boy's eyes and heart. And wherever they flew, the sweet strong perfume of the elder-tree floated round them. The little boy could smell the roses in the gardens he flew past, and the fresh beech-trees; but the elder was the sweetest of all, for the flowers lay on the little maiden's heart, where, in their flight, he so often leaned his head.

'How beautiful is spring!' cried the little girl, as they stood together among the fresh green of the beech-wood, while the sweet-scented thyme grew at their feet, and the pale-tinted anemones looked their loveliest amid the soft greens of the grass. 'Oh, would it were always spring!'

'How beautiful is summer!' said she again, as they flew by a castle telling of olden times, and saw the high walls and pointed gables mirrored in the moat beneath, where the swans were floating, and peeped up the cool green avenues. A sea of green corn waved to and fro in the fields. Tiny red and yellow blossoms peeped out of the ditches, and the hedges were covered with wild hops and white bindweed. In the evening the moon rose large and round, and the meadows were odorous with the scent of haystacks. Such scenes are never to be forgotten.

'How beautiful is autumn!' said the little maiden also. The sky seemed higher, and of a deeper blue; the woods became flushed with the richest crimsons, greens, and yellows. The hounds dashed by in full cry; flocks of wild fowl flew screaming over the Hun's graves where the brambles twined round the old stones. Far away lay the deep blue sea, dotted with white sails. Old women, girls, and children sat in a barn, picking hops and putting them into a great cask. The young and the old told stories of fairies and enchantments. What could be pleasanter than this?

'How beautiful is winter!' she said. The trees stood around them all covered with hoar-frost. The snow crackled beneath the feet as if every one had on new boots, and, one after another, stars shot across the sky. The Christmas-tree was lighted up in the parlour; everybody had had presents given him, and everybody was in good humour. In the farm-houses could be heard the sound of fiddles; and there were games for apples, so that even the poorest child might say, 'How beautiful is winter!'

And beautiful indeed were all the scenes that the fairy maiden showed to the little boy, and still the elder-perfume floated round them, and ever over them waved the red flag with the white cross under which the old mariner had sailed. And the boy, now grown to be a youth, felt that he must go out to seek his fortune in the world. At their parting the maiden took the cluster of elder-blossoms from her bosom, and gave it to him. And he kept it carefully between the leaves of his hymn-book, and when he was in foreign lands he never took up the book but it opened upon the place where the flowers of memory lay, and the oftener he looked at it the fresher, he fancied, it became. He seemed, while he looked at it, to breathe the sweetness of his native woods, and a hundred fair visions of the past floated unbidden through his mind.

Many years had passed, and he was now an old man

"How beautiful is winter!"

sitting with his old wife under a flowering tree. They held each other by the hand, and they talked of old times, and of their golden wedding-day. The little maiden, with the blue eyes and the elder-blossoms in her hair, sat on the tree above, and nodded to them, saying, 'Today is your golden wedding-day!' and then she took two flower clusters out of her hair and kissed them twice. At the first kiss they shone like silver; at the second, like gold, and when she had set them on the two old people's heads, each cluster became a gold crown. And thus they sat like a King and Queen, under the fragrant elder-tree, and the old man began to tell his wife the story about Elder-Tree Mother. It had been told him when a little boy, and it seemed to them both that great part of the story was very like their own, and they liked that part far the best.

'Yes, so it is!' said the little maiden in the tree. 'Some call me Elder-Tree Mother, others call me a Dryad, but my proper name is Memory. Here I sit in the tree whilst it grows and grows; I never forget, I remember all things well. Now let me see if you still have your flower safe?'

The old man opened his hymn-book, and there lay the elder-flower, as fresh as though it had but just been laid between the leaves. Memory nodded her head, and the two old people with their gold crowns sat under the tree, their faces flushed with the red evening sunlight. They closed their eyes, and then—and then—why, then there was an end of the tale.

The little boy lay in his bed; he did not rightly know whether he had been dreaming all this, or whether it had been told him. The tea-pot stood on the table, but no elder-tree was growing out of it, and his friend, the old story-teller, was just on the point of going out at the door. Whilst the boy was rubbing his eyes he was gone.

'How beautiful that was!' said the little boy. 'Mother, I have been to the warm countries.'

'Yes, I have no doubt of that!' replied the mother; 'after you had drunk two full cups of hot elder-tea, you were likely enough to get into the warm countries!' And she covered him up well for fear he should get chilled. 'You have had a good sound sleep while I sat disputing with him as to whether it were a fairy tale, or a real, true history.'

'And where is Elder-Tree Mother?' asked the boy.

'She is in the tea-pot,' said his mother, 'and there she may stay.'

THE WILD SWANS

Far, far away, in the land to which the swallows fly in our winter-time, there dwelt a King who had eleven sons and one daughter, named Elise. The eleven brothers were Princes, and went to school with stars on their breasts and swords by their sides; they wrote on golden copy-books with diamond pens, and learnt by heart just as they read. In short, it was easy to see that they were Princes. Their sister Elise used to sit upon a little glass stool, and had a picture-book which had cost the half of a kingdom. Oh, the children were so happy! But happy they were not to remain always.

Their father, who was the King of the whole country, married a wicked Queen who was not at all kind to the poor children. They found this out on the first day after the marriage. There were great festivities at the palace; and the children played at receiving company, but, instead of letting them have, as usual, as many cakes and burnt apples as were left, the Queen gave them only some sand in a tea-cup, and told them to play at make-believe with that.

The week after, she sent the little Elise to be brought up by some peasants in the country, and before long she told the King so many falsehoods about the poor Princes, that he would have nothing more to do with them.

'Away, out into the world, and take care of yourselves,' said the wicked Queen; 'fly away in the form of great speechless birds.' But she could not make them ugly, as she wished to do, for they were changed into eleven white Swans. Sending forth a strange cry, they flew out of the palace windows, over the park and over the wood.

It was still early in the morning when they passed the peasant's cottage where Elise lay sleeping. They hovered over the roof, stretched their long necks, and flapped their wings; but no one either heard or saw them, so they were forced to fly away. They flew up to the clouds and out into the wide world, far away into the dark forest, which stretched as far as the seashore.

Poor little Elise stood in the peasant's cottage, playing with a green leaf, for she had no other plaything. She pricked a hole in the leaf and peeped through it at the sun, and then she fancied she saw her brothers' bright eyes, and whenever the warm sunbeams shone full upon her cheeks, she thought of her brothers' kisses.

One day was just like another. When the wind blew through the thick hedge of rose-trees in front of the house, she would whisper to the roses, 'Who is more beautiful than you?' And the roses would shake their heads and say, 'Elise.' And when the peasant's wife sat on Sundays at the door of her cottage reading her hymn-book, the wind would rustle the leaves and say to the book, 'Who is more pious than you?' And the hymn-book would answer, 'Elise.' And what the roses and the hymn-book said, was no more the truth.

When she was fifteen years old she had to go home, and when the Queen saw how beautiful she was, she hated her more than ever, and would willingly have turned her, like her brothers, into a Wild Swan; but she dared not do so, because the King wished to see his daughter.

Early one morning the Queen went into the bathroom which was made of marble, and fitted up with soft pillows and the gayest carpets. She took three toads with her and kissed them, and said to one, 'When Elise comes to the bath settle thou upon her head that she may become dull and sleepy like thee.' 'Settle thou upon her forehead,' said she to another, 'and let her become ugly like thee, so that her father may not know her again.' And 'Do thou place thyself upon her bosom,' whispered she to the third, 'that her heart may become evil, and a torment to herself.' She then put the toads into clear water, which immediately turned green, and having called Elise, took off her clothes and made her get into the bath. As she dipped her head under the water, one toad settled among her hair, another on her forehead, and the third upon her bosom. But Elise seemed not at all aware of it; and when she rose up three poppies were seen swimming on the water. Had not the animals been poisonous and kissed by a witch, they would have been changed into roses because they had rested on Elise's head and heart. She was too good for magic to have any power over her.

When the Queen perceived this, she rubbed walnut juice all over the maiden's skin, so that it became quite swarthy, smeared a nasty salve over her lovely face, and entangled her long thick hair, till it was impossible to recognize the beautiful Elise. When her father saw her, he was shocked, and said she could not be his daughter. No one knew her but the mastiff and the swallows; and they were only poor animals and could not say anything.

Poor Elise wept, and thought of her eleven brothers who were all away. In great distress she stole away and wandered the whole day over fields and marshes, till she came to the great forest. She knew not where to go, but she was so sad, and longed so much to see her brothers, who like herself had been driven out into the world, that she made up her mind to seek for them and find them.

She had not been long in the forest when night came on, and she lost her way amid the darkness. So she lay down on the soft moss, said her evening prayer, and leaned her head against the trunk of a tree. It was very still in the forest; the air was mild, and from the grass and mould around gleamed the green lights of many hundred glow-worms; and when Elise touched one of the branches hanging over her, bright insects fell down upon her like falling stars.

All the night long she dreamed of her brothers. It seemed to her that they were all children again, played together, wrote with diamond pens upon golden copy-books, and looked at the pictures in the beautiful book that had cost half a kingdom. But they did not as formerly make straight strokes and pot-hooks upon the copy-books.

No; they wrote of the noble deeds they had done, and the strange things they had seen. In the picture-book, too, everything seemed alive; the birds sang, and the men and women stepped from the pages and talked to Elise and her brothers, jumping back into their places, however, when she turned over the leaves, so that the pictures did not get confused.

When Elise awoke, the sun was already high in the heavens. She could not see it, for the tall trees twined their thickly-leaved branches so closely together that, as the sunbeams played upon them, they looked like a golden veil waving to and fro. The air was fragrant, and the bird almost perched upon Elise's shoulders. She heard the noise of water, and when she went towards it she found a pool, formed by several springs, with the prettiest pebbles at the bottom. Bushes were growing thickly round, but the deer had trodden a broad path through them, and by this path Elise went down to the water's edge. The water was so clear that had not the boughs and bushes around been moved to and fro by the wind she might have fancied they were painted upon the smooth surface, so distinctly was each little leaf mirrored upon it, whether glowing in the sunlight or lying in the shade.

When Elise saw her own face in the water she was frightened, so brown and ugly did it look; but when she wetted her little hand, and rubbed her brow and eyes, the white skin again appeared. So she took off her clothes, stepped into the fresh water and bathed herself, and in the whole world there was not a king's daughter more beautiful than she then appeared.

After she had again dressed herself, and had braided her long hair, she went to the bubbling spring, caught some water in the hollow of her hand and drank it, and then wandered farther into the forest. She knew not where she was going, but she thought of her brothers, and of the good God who, she felt, would never forsake her. He it was who made the wild apples grow to feed the hungry, and who showed her a tree whose boughs bent under the weight of their fruit. She made her noonday meal under the shade of this tree, then propped up the boughs, and walked on into the gloomiest depths of the forest. It was so still that she could hear her own footsteps, and the rustling of each little withered leaf that was crushed beneath her feet. Not a bird was to be seen, not a sunbeam penetrated the thick foliage; and the tall stems of the trees stood so close together, that when she looked straight before her she seemed enclosed by trellis-work upon trellis-work. Oh! there was a solitariness in this forest such as Elise had never known before.

And the night was so dark! not a single glow-worm sent forth its light from the moss. Sorrowfully she lay down to sleep. Then it seemed to her as though the boughs above her opened, and she saw the angels of God smiling down upon her, and a thousand little cherubs all around him. When she awoke in the morning she could not tell whether this was a dream, or whether it had really happened.

She walked on a little farther, and met an old woman with a basket full of berries. The old woman gave her some of the berries, and Elise asked if she had not seen eleven Princes ride through the wood.

'No,' said the old woman, 'but I saw yesterday eleven Swans with golden crowns on their heads swim down the brook near here.'

Then she led Elise on a little farther to a sloping bank at the foot of which ran a little brook. The trees on each side stretched their long leafy branches towards each other, and where they could not unite naturally the roots had torn themselves from the earth, so that the branches might mingle their foliage as they hung over the water.

Elise bade the old woman farewell, and wandered by the side of the stream till she came to the place where it reached the open sea.

The great, the beautiful sea lay before the maiden's eyes, but not a ship, not a boat was to be seen. How was she to go on? She noticed how the numberless little stones on the shore had all been washed into a round form by the waves; glass, iron, stone, everything that lay scattered there had been moulded into shape, and yet the water which had done this much was softer than Elise's delicate little hand.

'The water rolls on unweariedly,' said she, 'till it smooths all that is hard; I will be no less unwearied! Thank you for the lesson you have given me, ye bright rolling waves; some day, my heart tells me, you shall carry me to my dear brothers!'

Upon the wet sea-grass lay eleven white swan-feathers. Elise gathered them up and put them together. Drops of water hung about them, whether dew or tears she could not tell. She was quite alone on the seashore, but she did not mind that, for the sea was full of interest to her; it was always moving, always changing, always new, and so gave her more pleasure in a few hours than the gentle inland waters could have given in a whole year. When a black cloud passed over the sky, it seemed as if the sea would say, 'I too can look dark'; and then the wind would blow and the waves fling out their white foam; but when the clouds shone with a bright red tint, and the winds were asleep, the sea became like a rose-leaf now green, now white. Yet however smooth its glassy surface was, there was always a slight motion near the shore as the waves rose and fell like the breast of a sleeping child.

At sunset Elise saw eleven Wild Swans with golden crowns on their heads fly towards the land; they flew one behind another, looking like a long white ribbon. Elise climbed the slope from the shore and hid herself behind a bush. The Swans came down close to her, and flapped their long white wings.

As the sun sank beneath the water, the Swan's feathers fell off, and beside her stood eleven handsome Princes, her brothers. She uttered a loud cry, for although they were very much changed, Elise knew and felt that they must be her brothers. Then she threw herself into their arms, calling them by their names, and the Princes were very happy to see their sister, now grown so tall and so beautiful! They laughed and wept, and soon told each other how wickedly their step-mother had acted towards them.

'We brothers,' said the eldest, 'fly or swim as long as the sun is in the sky, but when it sets we appear again in our human form; we are therefore bound to look out for a safe resting-place before sunset, for if we were flying among the clouds at the time we should fall down into the sea when we recovered our human shape. We do not dwell here. A land quite as beautiful as this lies on the other side of the sea, but it is far off. To reach it we have to cross the deep waters, and there is no island midway on which we may rest at night. One little solitary rock rises from the waves, and upon it we only find room enough to stand side by side. There we spend the night in our human form; and when the sea is rough the foam dashes over us. But we thank God even for this rock, for without it we should never be able to visit our dear native country. Only once in the year are we allowed to make this visit to our home. We require two of the longest days for our flight, and can remain here only eleven days, during which time we fly over the large forest, whence we can see the palace in which we were born, where our father dwells, and the tower of the church in which our mother was buried. Here even the trees and bushes seem of kin to us. The wild horses still race over the plain as in the days of our childhood. The charcoal-burner still sings the same old tunes to which we used to dance in our youth. This is our fatherland to which we are drawn by ties of love; and here we have found thee, thou dear little sister! We have yet two days longer to stay here, and then we must fly over the sea to a land beautiful indeed, but not our fatherland. How shall we take thee with us? we have neither ship nor boat!'

'How can I break this spell?' said the sister. And so they went on talking almost the whole of the night. They slept only a few hours.

Elise was awakened by the rustling of wings, and saw the Swans fluttering above her. Her brothers were again changed into Swans. For some time they flew round in wider and wider circles, till at last they flew far away. One of them remained behind; it was the youngest. He laid his head in her lap and she stroked his white wings; they remained the whole day together. Towards evening the others came back, and when the sun was set, again they stood on the firm ground in their natural form.

'Tomorrow we shall fly away,' they said, 'and may not return for a year, but we cannot leave you here. Have you courage to go with us? Our arms are strong enough to bear you through the forest, and will not our wings be strong enough to fly with you over the sea?'

'Yes, take me with you,' said Elise.

They spent the whole night in weaving a mat of the pliant willow bark and the tough rushes, and their mat was thick and strong. Elise lay down upon it, and when the sun had risen, and the brothers had been turned again into Wild Swans, they seized the mat with their beaks and flew up high among the clouds with their dear sister. She was still sleeping, and, as the sunbeams shone full upon her face, one of the Swans flew over her head and shaded her with his broad wings.

They were already far from land when Elise awoke. She thought she was still dreaming, so strange did it seem to her to feel herself being carried so high up in the air over the sea. By her side lay a cluster of pretty ripe berries and a bundle of sweet roots. Her youngest brother had gathered them for her and laid them there, and she thanked him with a smile, for she knew him as the Swan who flew over her head and shaded her with his wings.

They soared so high that the first ship they saw beneath them seemed like a white sea-gull hovering over the water. Elise saw behind her a large cloud, which looked like a mountain, and on it were gigantic shadows of herself and the eleven Swans; altogether it formed a picture more beautiful than any she had ever yet seen. Soon, however, the sun rose higher, the cloud was left behind, and the shadowy picture disappeared.

The whole day they flew on like a winged arrow through

the air, but yet they went slower than usual, for they had their sister to carry. There seemed a storm brewing, and the evening was drawing near. Anxiously did Elise watch the sun. It was setting, and still the solitary rock could not be seen. It appeared to her that the Swans plied their wings faster and faster. Alas! it would be her fault if her brothers did not arrive at the rock in time. They would become human beings when the sun set, and must fall into the sea and be drowned. She prayed to God most fervently. Still no rock was to be seen. The black clouds drew nearer, and gusts of wind told of a coming storm, while from a mass of clouds that seemed to move forward like a leaden threatening wave flash after flash of lightning broke forth.

The sun was now on the rim of the sea. Elise's heart beat fast; the Swans shot downward so swiftly that she thought she must fall, but another moment they began to soar again. The sun was half sunk beneath the water, but now she saw the little rock below her; it looked like a seal's head when he raises it just above the water. The sun was sinking fast. It seemed scarce larger than a star as her foot touched the hard ground, and in a moment it vanished altogether, like the last spark on a burnt piece of paper. Arm in arm her brothers stood around her; there was just room for her and them. The sea beat wildly against the rock, flinging over them a shower of foam. The sky seemed ablaze with the continual flashes, and one clap of thunder followed close on another, but sister and brothers kept firm hold of each other's hands. They sang a psalm, and their psalm gave them comfort and courage.

By daybreak the air was pure and still; and, as soon as the sun rose, the Swans flew away with Elise from the rock. The sea was still rough, and from the clouds the white foam that crested the blackish-green waves looked as if millions of swans were swimming on the waters.

As day advanced, Elise saw before her floating in the air a range of mountains, with masses of glittering ice on their summits. In their midst stood a castle at least a mile in length, with rows of columns, one above another, while around it grew palm-trees and gorgeous-looking flowers as large as mill-wheels. She asked if this was the land to which they were flying, but the Swans shook their heads, for what she saw was the beautiful ever-changing cloud castle of the fairy Morgana, which no human being can ever enter. Whilst Elise still bent her eyes upon it, mountains, trees, and castle all disappeared, and in their place stood twenty stately churches with high towers and pointed windows—she fancied she heard the organ play, but it was only the murmur of the sea. As they drew nearer to these churches they too changed into a large fleet sailing under them. She looked down and saw it was only a sea-mist passing rapidly over the water. Such strange scenes kept floating before her eyes, till at last she saw the actual land to which they were going with its blue mountains, its cedar woods, its towns, and castles. Long before sunset Elise sat down among the mountains, in front of a large cavern where delicate young creepers grew so thickly around that the ground appeared covered with gay embroidered carpets.

'Now we shall see what thou wilt dream of tonight!' said her youngest brother, as he showed her the chamber where she was to sleep.

'Oh that I could dream how you might be freed from the spell!' said she; and she could think of nothing else. She prayed most earnestly for God's help, nay, even in her dreams she continued praying, and it appeared to her that she was flying up high in the air towards the castle of the fairy Morgana. The fairy came forward to meet her, radiant and beautiful, and yet she thought she looked like the old woman who had given her berries in the forest, and told her of the Swans with golden crowns.

'You can release your brothers,' said she; 'but have you courage and patience enough? The water is indeed softer than your delicate hands, and yet can mould the hard stones to its will, but then it cannot feel the pain which your tender fingers will feel; it has no heart, and cannot suffer the anxiety and grief which you must suffer. Do you see these stinging-nettles I have in my hand? There are many round the cave where you are sleeping; only those that grow there or on the graves in the churchyard are of use, remember that! You must pluck them though they sting your hand; you must trample on them with your feet, and get yarn from them, and with this yarn you must weave eleven shirts with long sleeves. When they are all made, throw them over the eleven Wild Swans, and the spell will be broken. But mark this: from the moment that you begin your work till it is completed, even should it occupy you for years, you must not speak a word. The first syllable that escapes your lips will fall like a dagger into the hearts of your brothers. On your tongue depends their life. Mark well all this!'

At the same moment the fairy touched Elise's hands with a nettle, which made them burn like fire, and Elise awoke. It was broad daylight, and close to her lay a nettle like the one she had seen in her dream. She fell upon her knees, thanked God, and then went out of the cave to begin her work. She plucked with her own delicate hands the ugly stinging-nettles. They burned large blisters on her hands and arms, but she bore the pain willingly in the hope of freeing her dear brothers. Then she trampled on the nettles with her naked feet, and spun the green yarn.

At sunset came her brothers. Elise's silence quite frightened them; they thought it must be the effect of some fresh spell of their wicked step-mother; but when they saw her blistered hands, they found out what their sister was doing for their sake. The youngest brother wept, and when his tears fell upon her hands, Elise felt no more pain, and the blisters disappeared.

The whole night she spent in her work, for she could not rest till she had released her brothers. All the following day she sat in her solitude, for the Swans had flown away; but never had time passed so quickly. One shirt was ready; and she now began the second.

Suddenly a hunting-horn echoed among the mountains and made her start with fear. The noise came nearer, she heard the hounds barking. In great terror she fled into the cave, bound up into a bundle the nettles she had gathered and combined, and sat down upon it.

She had just done so when a large dog sprang out from the bushes. Two others immediately followed; they barked loudly, ran away, and then returned. It was not long before the hunters stood in front of the cave. The handsomest among them was the King of that country; and he stepped up to Elise, for never had he seen a lovelier maiden.

'How came you here, beautiful child?' said he. Elise shook her head; she dared not speak, a word might have cost her the life of her brothers; and she hid her hands under her apron lest the King should see how she was suffering.

'Come with me,' said he. 'You must not stay here! If you are as good as you are beautiful, I will dress you in velvet and silk, I will put a gold crown upon your head, and you shall dwell in my palace!' So he lifted her upon his horse, while she wept and wrung her hands; but the King said, 'I only desire your happiness! You shall thank me for this some day!' and away he rode over mountains and valleys, holding her on his horse in front, whilst the other hunters followed. When the sun set, the King's capital with its churches and domes lay before them, and the King led Elise into the palace, where, in a high marble hall, fountains were playing, and the walls and ceiling were covered with the most beautiful paintings. But Elise cared not for all this splendour; she wept and mourned in silence, even whilst some female attendants dressed her in royal robes, wove costly pearls into her hair, and drew soft gloves over her blistered hands.

And now as she stood before them in her rich dress, her beauty was so dazzling, that the courtiers all bowed low before her, and the King chose her for his bride, although the Archbishop shook his head, and whispered that the 'beautiful lady of the wood was only a witch, who had blinded their eyes and bewitched the King's heart'.

But the King did not listen; he ordered that music should be played. The most costly dishes were served up, and the lovliest maidens danced round the bride. She was led through fragrant gardens into magnificent halls, but not a smile was seen to play upon her lips or beam from her eyes. She looked the very picture of grief. The King then opened a small room next her bedroom. The floor was covered with costly green tapestry, and looked exactly like the cave in which she had been found. On it lay the bundle of yarn which she had spun from the nettles, and by the wall hung the shirt she had made. One of the hunters had brought all this, thinking there must be something wonderful in it.

'Here you may dream of your former home,' said the King. 'Here is the work you were doing there. Amid all your present splendour it may sometimes give you pleasure to fancy yourself there again.'

When Elise saw what was so dear to her heart, she smiled, and the blood came back to her cheeks. She thought her brothers might still be freed from the spell, and she kissed the King's hand. He pressed her to his heart, and ordered the bells of all the churches in the city to be rung, to announce their marriage. The beautiful dumb maiden of the wood was to become the Queen of the land.

The Archbishop whispered evil words in the King's ear, but he paid no heed to them. He and Elise were married, and the Archbishop himself was obliged to put the crown upon her head. In his rage he pressed the narrow rim so firmly on her forehead that it hurt her; but a heavier weight of sorrow for her brothers lay upon her heart, and she did not feel bodily pain. She was still silent, because a single word would have killed her brothers; but her eyes beamed with heartfelt love to the King, so good and handsome, who had done so much to make her happy. She loved him more and more every day. Oh! how she wished she might tell him her sorrows; but she must remain silent, she could not speak until her work was finished! So she stole away every night, and went into the little room that was fitted up like the cave. There she worked at her shirts;

but by the time she had begun the seventh, all her yarn was spent.

She knew that the nettles she needed grew in the churchyard, but she must gather them herself; and how to get them she knew not.

'Oh, what is the pain in my fingers compared with the anguish my heart suffers!' thought she. 'I must venture to the churchyard; the good God will still watch over me!'

Fearful as though she were about to do something wrong, one moonlight night she crept down to the garden, and through the long avenues into the lonely road leading to the churchyard. She saw sitting on one of the broadest tombstones a number of ugly old witches. They took off their ragged clothes as if they were going to bathe, and digging with their long lean fingers into the fresh grass, drew up the dead bodies and devoured the flesh. Elise was obliged to pass close by them, and the witches fixed their wicked eyes upon her; but she repeated her prayer, gathered the stinging-nettles, and took them back with her into the palace. One person only had seen her. It was the Archbishop; he was awake when others slept. Now he felt sure that all was not right about the Queen: she must be a witch, who had, by her magic, won the hearts of the King and all the people.

In the Confessional he told the King what he had seen, and what he feared; and when the slanderous words came from his lips, the sculptured images of the saints shook their heads as though they would say, 'It is untrue, Elise is innocent!' But the Archbishop explained the omen quite otherwise; he thought it was a testimony against her, and that the holy images shook their heads at hearing of her sin.

Two large tears rolled down the King's cheeks; and he returned home in doubt. He pretended to sleep at night, though sleep never visited him; and he noticed that Elise rose from her bed every night, and every time he followed her secretly and saw her enter her little room.

His face grew darker every day. Elise perceived it,

though she did not know the cause. She was much pained; and besides, what did she not suffer in her heart for her brothers! Her bitter tears ran down on the royal velvet and purple, looking like bright diamonds; and all who saw the grandeur that surrounded her wished themselves in her place. She had now nearly finished her work, only one shirt was wanting. Unfortunately, yarn was wanting also; she had not a single nettle left. Once more, only this one time, she must go the the churchyard and gather a few handfuls. She shuddered when she thought of the solitary walk and of the horrid witches, but her resolution was as firm as her trust in God.

Elise went, and the King and the Archbishop followed her. They saw her disappear at the churchyard door; and when they came nearer they saw the witches sitting on the tombstones as Elise had seen them; and the King turned away, for he believed her whose head had rested on his bosom that very evening to be amongst them. 'Let the people judge her!' said he. And the people condemned her to be burnt.

She was now dragged from the King's splendid palace into a dark, damp prison, where the wind whistled through the grated window. Instead of velvet and silk, they gave her the bundle of nettles she had gathered. On that she had to lay her head, and the shirts she had woven had to serve her as mattress and counterpane. But they could not have given her anything more welcome to her; and she continued her work, at the same time praying earnestly to God. The boys sang shameful songs about her in front of her prison; not a soul comforted her with one word of love.

Towards evening she heard the rustling of Swans' wings at the grating. It was the youngest of her brothers, who had at last found her, and she sobbed aloud for joy, although she knew that probably she has only one night to live; but then her work was almost finished and her brothers were near.

The Archbishop came in to spend the last hour with her as he had promised the King he would; but she shook her head and begged him with looks and signs to go away; for this night she must finish her work, or all she had suffered, her pain, her anxiety, her sleepless nights, would be in vain. The Archbishop went away with many angry words; but poor Elise knew herself to be perfectly innocent, and went on with her work.

Little mice ran busily about and dragged the nettles to her feet, wishing to help her; and a thrush perched on the iron bars of the window, and sang all night as merrily as he could, that she might not lose courage.

An hour before sunrise the eleven brothers stood before the palace gates, and begged to be shown to the King. But it could not be, they were told; it was still night, the King was asleep, and they dared not wake him. They prayed, they threatened in vain. The guard came up; at last the King himself stepped out to ask what was the matter; but at that moment the sun rose, the brothers could be seen no longer, and eleven white Swans flew away over the palace.

The people poured forth from the gates of the city to see the witch burnt. One wretched horse drew the cart in which Elise sat. She wore a coarse frock of sackcloth, her beautiful long hair hung loosely over her shoulders, her cheeks were of a deathly paleness; but her lips moved gently, and her fingers wove the green yarn, for even on her way to her cruel death, she did not give up her work. The ten shirts lay at her feet, she was now labouring to complete the eleventh. The crowd insulted her.

'Look at the witch, how she mutters! she has no psalm-book in her hand,—no, there she sits with her hateful juggling! Tear it from her, tear it into a thousand pieces!'

And they all crowded about her, and were on the point of snatching away the shirts, when eleven white Swans came flying towards the cart, settled all round her, and flapped their wings. The crowd gave way in terror.

'It is a sign from Heaven! she is certainly innocent!' whispered some; they dared not say so aloud.

The executioner now took hold of her hand to lift her

out of the cart, but she hastily threw the eleven shirts over the Swans, and eleven handsome Princes appeared in their place. The youngest had, however, only one arm, and a wing instead of the other, for one sleeve in his shirt had not been quite finished.

'Now I may speak,' said she; 'I am innocent!'

And the people who had seen what had happened bowed before her as before a saint. She, however, sank lifeless in her brothers' arms; suspense, fear, and grief had quite exhausted her.

'Yes, she is innocent,' said her eldest brother, and he told their wonderful story. Whilst he spoke a fragrance as from millions of roses spread itself around, for every piece of wood in the funeral pile had taken root and sent forth branches, and a hedge of blooming red roses surrounded Elise, and above all the other blossomed a flower of a dazzling white colour, bright as a star. The King plucked it and laid it on Elise's bosom, and then she awoke with peace and joy in her heart.

And all the church bells began to ring of their own accord, and birds flew to the spot in swarms, and there was a joyous procession back to the palace, such as no king has ever seen equalled.

THE RED SHOES

There was once a little girl, very pretty and delicate, but so poor that in summer she always went barefoot, and in winter wore large wooden shoes that made her little ankles quite red and sore.

In the same village lived an old shoemaker's wife. One day she made out of some old pieces of red cloth a pair of little shoes. They were clumsy certainly, but they fitted the little girl fairly well, and she gave them to her. The little girl's name was Karen.

It was on the day of her mother's funeral that the red shoes were given to Karen. They were not at all proper for mourning, but she had no others, and in them she walked with bare legs behind the poor deal coffin.

Just then a large old carriage rolled by. In it sat a large old lady who saw the little girl and pitied her, and she said to the priest, 'Give me the little girl, and I will take care of her.'

Karen thought it was for the sake of the red shoes that the old lady had taken a fancy to her; but the old lady thought them frightful, and so they were burnt. And Karen was dressed very neatly, and was taught to read and to work; and people told her she was pretty. But the mirror said, 'You are more than pretty; you are beautiful!'

One day the Queen with her little daughter passed through the town where Karen lived, and all the people, Karen amongst them, crowded in front of the palace, whilst the little princess stood, dressed in white, at a window, for every one to see her. She wore neither train nor gold crown; but on her feet were pretty red morocco shoes—much prettier indeed than those the shoemaker's wife had made for little Karen. Nothing in the world could be compared with these red shoes!

Karen was now old enough to be confirmed. She was to have a new frock and new shoes. The rich shoemaker in the town took the measure of her little foot. He took the measure in his own room where there was a large glass case full of neat shoes and shining boots. They looked very pretty, but the old lady, whose sight was not very good, did not notice them much. Amongst the shoes was a pair of red ones, just like those worn by the Princess. The shoemaker said they had been made for a Count's daughter but did not fit.

'They are of polished leathers' said the old lady; 'see how they shine!'

'Yes, they shine beautifully!' exclaimed Karen. And as the shoes fitted her, they were bought. But the old lady did not know that they were red, or she would never have suffered Karen to go to confirmation in them. But Karen did go. Everybody looked at her feet, and as she walked up the nave to the chancel it seemed to her that even the stone figures on the tombstones, and the portraits of the pastors and their wives with their stiff ruffs and long black robes, fixed their eyes on her red shoes. When she knelt before the altar she thought only of them; even when the clergyman laid his hand on her head, and when he spoke of her baptism, of her covenant with God, and of how she must remember that she was now a full-grown Christian. The organ sent forth its deep, solemn tones, the children's sweet voices mingled with those of the choristers, but Karen still thought only of her red shoes.

That afternoon, when the old lady was told that Karen had worn red shoes at her confirmation, she was vexed, and told Karen that for the future when she went to church, she must wear black shoes, were they ever so old.

On the next Sunday Karen was to make her first communion. She looked first at the red shoes, then at the black, then at the red again, and—put them on.

It was beautiful sunshiny weather, so Karen and the old lady walked to church through the corn-fields, for the road was dusty.

At the church door stood an old soldier with a strange reddish-coloured beard. He was leaning on crutches, and he bowed almost to the earth, and asked the old lady if he might wipe the dust off her shoes. Karen put out her little foot also. 'Oh, what pretty dancing-shoes!' said the old soldier; 'mind you do not let them slip off when you dance;' and he passed his hands over them.

The old lady gave the soldier some money, and then went with Karen into Church.

Again every one looked at Karen's red shoes; and all the carved figures bent their gaze upon them. And when Karen knelt before the altar, the red shoes still floated before her eyes. She thought of them and of them only, and she forgot to join in the hymn of praise—she forgot to repeat the Lord's Prayer.

At last all the people came out of church, and the old lady got into her carriage. Karen was lifting her foot to follow, when the old soldier standing in the porch cried, 'Only look, what pretty dancing-shoes!' And then Karen found she could not help dancing a few steps. And after she had begun, her feet kept moving of themselves as though the shoes had a power over them. She danced round the churchyard and could not stop. The coachman was obliged to run after her, take hold of her and lift her into the carriage; but even then the feet kept on dancing, so that the good old lady got many a hard kick. At last the shoes were taken off, and the feet had rest.

Then the shoes were put away in a press, but Karen could not help going to look at them every now and then.

After a while the old lady lay ill in bed, and the doctor said she would never get better. She needed careful nursing, and who should have been her nurse and constant attendant but Karen? But there was to be a grand ball in the town, and Karen was invited. She thought of the dying old lady, she looked at the red shoes, and then she thought there could be no harm in putting them on. Then she went to the ball and began to dance. But when she wanted to move to the right, the shoes bore her to the left; and when she would dance up the room, the shoes danced down the room, danced down the stairs, through the streets, and through the gates of the town. She danced on in spite of herself, till she danced into the dark wood.

Something shone through the trees. She thought at first it must be the moon shining through the mist. Then she saw a face; it was the old soldier with the red beard. He sat there nodding at her, and repeating, 'See what pretty dancing-shoes they are!'

She was frightened, and tried to pull off her red shoes, but they were stuck fast to her feet. She tore off her stockings but the shoes seemed to have grown on to her feet. She felt compelled to go on dancing over field and meadow, in rain and in sunshine, by night and by day. It was most terrible at night. She danced across the open churchyard. The dead do not dance, they have something better to do. She would fain have sat down on the poor man's grave, where the bitter ferns grew, but for her there was neither rest nor quiet. She danced past the open church door, and there she saw an angel, clad in long white robes, and with wings that reached from her shoulders to the ground. His face was grave and stern, and in his hand he held a bright, glittering sword.

'Dance on,' said he; 'dance on, in thy red shoes, till thou art pale and cold, and thy skin shrinks and shrivels up like a skeleton's. Thou shalt dance still, from door to door, and wherever proud, vain children live thou shalt knock, so that they may hear thee and be afraid. Dance shalt thou, dance on——'

'Mercy!' cried Karen. But she heard not the angel's answer, for the shoes carried her through the gate, into the fields, along highways and byways; and still she had to dance on.

One morning she danced past a door she knew well. She heard psalm-singing within, and saw a coffin, strewn with flowers, borne out. Then Karen knew that the good old lady was dead, and she felt herself a thing forsaken by men, and condemned by the Angel of God.

Still, on she felt forced to dance, even into the dark night. The shoes bore her through thorns and briers, till her limbs were torn and bleeding. Then she danced across the heath to a little lonely house where she knew the headsman lived; and she tapped with her fingers against the panes, crying:

'Come out! come out! I cannot come in for I must dance.'

And the headsman said, 'Surely you do not know who I am! I cut off the heads of wicked men; and I notice that my axe is quivering.'

'Do not cut off my head,' said Karen, 'for then I could not live to repent of my sin; but cut off my feet with the red shoes.'

Then she confessed all her sins, and the headsman cut off her feet with the red shoes on them; and the shoes with those little feet in them danced away over the fields, and into the deep forests.

Then the headsman made her a pair of wooden feet, and cut down some branches to serve as crutches, and he taught her the psalm which the penitents sing. And she kissed the hand that held the axe, and limped away over the heath. 'Now I have certainly suffered quite enough through the red shoes,' thought Karen, 'I will go to church and let people see me once more.' And she went as fast as she could to the church porch; but as she drew near it, the red shoes danced before her, and she was frightened and turned her back.

All that week she was sorrowful and shed many bitter tears. Then when Sunday came, she said to herself, 'Now I have suffered and striven enough; I dare say I am quite as good as many of those who are holding their heads so high in church.' So she took heart and went; but she did not get farther than the churchyard gate, for there again she saw the red shoes dancing before her, and in great terror she turned back, and repented more deeply than ever of her sinful pride.

Then she went to the pastor's house, and begged that

some work might be given her, promising to work hard and
do all she could even without wages. She only wanted a
roof to shelter her, she said, and to dwell with good people.
And the pastor's wife had pity on her, and took her into
her service. And Karen was grateful and industrious.

Every evening she sat silently listening to the pastor
while he read the Bible aloud. All the children loved her
but when she heard them talk about dress and finery, and,
about being as beautiful as a queen, she would sorrowfully
shake her head.

Next Sunday all the pastor's household went to church;
and they asked her to go too; but she sighed, and looked
with tears in her eyes upon her crutches.

When they were all gone, she went into her own little
room, which was just large enough to hold a bed and a
chair, and there she sat with her psalm-book in her hand
and, as she read in a humble and devout spirit, the wind
wafted to her the sound of the organ from the church,
and she lifted up her tearful face and prayed, 'O God,
help me!'

Then the sun shone brightly, and before her stood the
white-robed Angel of God, the same whom she had seen on
that night of horror at the church porch. But he no longer
held in his hand a threatening sword; he carried instead a
lovely green branch covered with roses. With this he
touched the ceiling, which at once rose to a great height,
and a bright gold star glittered on the spot the green branch
had touched. He touched the walls too, and they opened
wide, and Karen saw the organ, the old monuments, and
the congregation all sitting in their richly carved seats and
singing from their psalm-books.

For the church had come home to the poor girl in her
narrow room, or rather the room had grown a church to
her. She sat with the rest of the pastor's servants, and,
when the psalm was ended, they looked up and nodded to
her, saying, 'You did well to come, Karen!'

'It was through mercy I came,' said she.

And then the organ pealed forth again, and with it the

children's voices in the choir rose clear and sweet. The sunbeams streamed through the windows and fell bright and warm on Karen's seat. Her heart was so full of sunshine, of peace and gladness, that it broke; and her soul flew upon a sunbeam to her Father in heaven, where not a look of reproach awaited her, not a word was breathed of the red shoes.

THE CONSTANT TIN SOLDIER

There were once five and twenty tin soldiers, all brothers, for all had been made out of one old tin spoon. They carried muskets in their arms, and held themselves very upright, and their uniforms were red and blue. The first words they heard in this world were, 'Tin soldiers!' It was a little boy who uttered them, when the lid was taken off the box where they lay; and he clapped his hands with delight. They had been given to him because it was his birthday. Then he set them out on the table.

The soldiers were like each other to a hair; all but one, who had only one leg, because he had been made last, when there was not quite enough tin left. He stood as firmly, however, upon his one leg as the others did upon their two; and it is this one-legged tin soldier's fortunes that seem to us worthy of being told.

On the table where the tin soldiers stood there were other playthings, but the most charming of them all was a pretty pasteboard castle. Through its little windows one could look into the rooms. In front of the castle stood some tiny trees, clustering round a little mirror intended to represent a lake. Some waxen swans swam on the lake and were reflected in it.

All this was very pretty, but prettiest of all was a little lady standing in the open doorway of the castle. She, too, was cut out of pasteboard, but she had on a frock of the softest muslin, and a narrow sky-blue riband was flung across her shoulders like a scarf, and in the middle of this scarf was set a glittering tinsel rose. The little lady was a dancer, and she stretched out both her arms, and raised one of her legs so high in the air that the tin soldier could not see it, and thought she had, like himself, only one leg.

'That would be just the wife for me,' thought he, 'but then she is of too high a rank. She lives in a castle, and I have only a box; and even that is not my own, for all our five and twenty men live in it; so it is no place for her. Still, I must make her acquaintance,' Then he laid himself down at full length behind a snuff-box that stood on the table so that he had a full view of the delicate little lady still standing on one leg without losing her balance.

When evening came, all the other tin soldiers were put into the box, and the people of the house went to bed. Then the playthings began to have their own games; to pay visits, to fight battles, and to give balls. The tin soldiers rattled in the box, for they wished to play too, but the lid would not open. The nut-crackers cut capers, and the slate-pencil danced about on the table. There was such a noise that the canary woke up and began to talk too; but he always talked in verse. The only two who did not move from their places were the tin soldier and the dancer. She remained standing on the very tip of her toes, with outstretched arms; and he stood just as firmly on his one leg, never for a moment taking his eyes off her.

Twelve o'clock struck, and with a crash the lid of the snuff-box sprang open—there was no snuff in it, it was only a toy puzzle—and out jumped a little black conjurer. 'Tin soldier!' said the conjurer, 'please keep your eyes to yourself!'

But the tin soldier pretended not to hear.

'Well, just wait till tomorrow!' said the conjurer.

When the children got up next morning the tin soldier was placed on the window-ledge, and, whether the conjurer or the wind caused it, all at once the window flew open, and out fell the tin soldier, head foremost, from the third storey to the ground. It was a dreadful fall, for he fell head first into the street, and at last rested with his cap and bayonet stuck between two paving-stones, and with his one leg in the air.

The servant-maid and the little boy came downstairs directly to look for him; but though they very nearly trod on him they could not see him. If the tin soldier had but called out, 'Here I am!' they might easily have found him;

but he thought it would not be becoming for him to cry out, as he was in uniform.

Presently it began to rain; soon the drops were falling thicker, and there was a perfect downpour. When it was over, two little street arabs came by.

'Look,' said one, 'there is a tin soldier. Let him have a sail for once in his life.'

So they made a boat out of newspaper, and put the tin soldier into it. Away he sailed down the gutter, both the boys running along by the side of it and clapping their hands. The paper boat rocked to and fro, and every now and then was whirled round so quickly that the tin soldier became quite giddy. Still he did not move a muscle but looked straight before him, and held his musket tightly clasped.

All at once the boat was carried into a long drain, where the tin soldier found it as dark as in his own box.

'Where can I be going now?' thought he. 'It is all that conjurer's doing. Ah! if only the little maiden were sailing with me I would not mind its being twice as dark.'

Just then a great water-rat that lived in the drain darted out. 'Have you a passport?' asked the rat. 'Show me your passport!' But the tin soldier was silent, and held his musket tighter than ever. The boat sailed on, and the rat followed. How he gnashed his teeth, and cried out to the sticks and the straws: 'Stop him, stop him, he has not paid his toll; he has not even shown his passport.' But the stream grew stronger and stronger. The tin soldier could already catch a glimpse of the daylight where the tunnel ended, but at the same time he heard a roaring noise that might have made the boldest tremble. Where the tunnel ended, the water of the gutter fell into a great canal. This was as dangerous for the tin soldier as a waterfall would be for us.

The fall was now so close that he could no longer stand upright. The boat darted forward; the poor tin soldier held himself as stiffly as possible; so that no one could accuse him of having even blinked. The boat span round three or four times, and was filled with water to the brim; it must sink now.

The tin soldier stood up to his neck in water; but deeper and deeper sank the boat, and softer and softer grew the paper till the water stood over the soldier's head. He thought of the pretty little dancer whom he should never see again, and these words rang in his ears:—

> Fare on, thou soldier brave!
> Life must end in the grave.

The paper now split in two, and the tin soldier fell through the rent and was at once swallowed up by a large fish. Oh, how dark it was! darker even than in the tunnel and much narrower too! But the tin soldier was as constant as ever; and lay there at full length, still shouldering his arms.

The fish swam to and fro, and made the strangest movements, but at last he became quite still. After a while a flash of lightning seemed to dart through him and the daylight shone brightly, and some one cried out, 'I declare, here is the tin soldier!' The fish had been caught, taken to the market, sold and brought into the kitchen, where the servant-girl was cutting him up with a large knife. She seized the tin soldier by the middle with two of her fingers, and took him into the parlour, where every one was eager to see the wonderful man who had travelled in the maw of a fish. But the tin soldier was not proud.

They set him on the table, and—what strange things do happen in the world!—the tin soldier was in the very room in which he had been before. He saw the same children, the same everything on the table—among them the beautiful castle with the pretty little dancing maiden, who was still standing upon one leg, while she held the other high in the air; she too was constant. It quite touched the tin soldier; he could have found it in his heart to weep tin tears, but such weakness would have been unbecoming in a soldier. He looked at her and she looked at him, but neither spoke a word.

And now one of the boys took the soldier and threw him into the stove. He gave no reason for doing so; but no doubt it was the fault of the conjurer in the snuff-box.

The tin soldier now stood in a blaze of light. He felt extremely hot, but whether from the fire or from the flames of love he did not know. He had entirely lost his colour. Whether this was the result of his travels, or the effect of strong feeling, I know not. He looked at the little lady, and she looked at him, and he felt that he was melting; but, constant as ever, he still stood shouldering his arms. A door opened, and the draught caught the dancer; and, like a sylph, she flew straightway into the stove, to the tin soldier. Instantly she was in a blaze and was gone. The soldier was melted and dripped down among the ashes, and when the maid cleaned out the fireplace the next day she found his remains in the shape of a little tin heart. Of the dancer all that was left was the tinsel rose, and that was as black as coal.

THE ANGEL

'Whenever a good child dies, and Angel comes down to earth, takes the dead child in his arms, and, spreading out his large white wings, flies, with him over all the places that were dear to him in his lifetime. And the Angel gathers a handful of flowers, and takes them to God, that they may bloom even more beautifully in Heaven than they did upon earth. And the flower which pleases Him most receives a voice and is able to join in the song of the chorus of bliss.'

Thus spoke an Angel of God while carrying a dead child to Heaven, and the child listened as if in a dream. Then they flew over all those places where the child had formerly played, and they passed through gardens full of lovely flowers.

'Which flower shall we take with us and plant in Heaven?' asked the Angel.

Near by stood a fair slender rose-bush, but some wicked hand had broken the stem, so that the half-opened buds hung faded and withered on the branches that it trailed on the ground. 'Poor rose-tree!' said the child, 'let us take it, that it may bloom again in Heaven.'

And the Angel took it, and he kissed the child, and the little one half-opened his eyes. The Angel gathered many fine garden flowers, but he took also the meek little daisy and the wild heart's-ease.

'Now we have flowers enough!' said the child, but the Angel only nodded, and did not yet fly up to Heaven.

It was night and very still in the great town. They stayed there, and hovered over one of the narrowest streets where straw, ashes, and rubbish of all kinds lay scattered. There had been a removal that day, and on the ground were broken plates, bits of plaster, rags, fragments of old hats, and other things not pleasant to see.

Amidst this confusion the Angel pointed to the pieces of an old flower-pot, and to a lump of earth that had fallen out of it. The earth was only held together by the roots of a large withered field-flower, which had been thrown out into the street among the refuse.

'We will take this flower with us also,' said the Angel. 'I will tell you why as we are flying along.'

And they flew away, and the Angel spoke as follows:

'There once lived in a cellar, down in that narrow street, a poor, sick boy. He had been bed-ridden from his childhood. Now and then, perhaps, he was able to take a few turns up and down his little room on his crutches, but that was all. Sometimes, during the summer, the sunbeams would stream through his little cellar window; and then, the child would sit up, and when he felt the warm sun shining upon him, and could see the crimson blood in his thin wasted fingers as he held them up to the light, he would say, "Today I have been out!" He only knew of the bright green woods of spring from a neighbour's son bringing him the first fresh boughs of the beech-tree. These he would hold over his head, and then fancy he was under the shade of the beech-trees, with the birds warbling and the sun shining around him.

'One spring day the neighbour's son brought him some field-flowers, and among them was one with a root, so it was put into a flower-pot and placed at the window, close by the bed. And, being carefully planted, it grew, and put forth fresh shoots, and bore flowers every year. To the sick boy it was like a beautiful garden, his little treasure upon earth. He watered it and guarded it, and took care that every sunbeam that entered the little low window should fall upon the plant. And its flowers, with their soft colours and sweet smell, mingled with his dreams, and towards them he turned when he was dying. The child has now been a year with the blessed; and for a year the plant has stood by the window, faded and forgotten, and today it was thrown out among the rubbish into the street. And this is the flower which we have just now taken; for this poor, faded field-flower has given more pleasure than the most splendid blossoms in the garden of a queen.'

'But how do you know all this?' asked the child, whom the Angel was carrying to Heaven.

'I know it,' said the Angel, 'because I myself was that little sick boy who went upon crutches. Ought I not to know my own flower?'

Then the child opened its eyes, and looked into the Angel's bright and happy face; and in the same moment they were in Heaven.

And God gave the dead child wings like the Angel's, so that he could fly hand in hand with that one; and a voice was given to the poor, faded field-flower, and it sang with the angels round the great white throne, some very near, and others forming larger circles, farther and farther away, but all equally blessed.

And they all sang together—the angels, the good child, and the poor faded field-flower, which had lain among the rubbish of that dark and narrow street.

THE SHEPHERDESS AND THE
CHIMNEY-SWEEP

Have you ever seen an old-fashioned oak cabinet, black
with age and covered every inch of it with carved foliage
and curious figures? Just such a cabinet, an heirloom once
the property of its present mistress's great-grandmother,
stood in a parlour. It was covered from top to bottom with
carved roses and tulips, and little stag's heads with long
branching antlers peered forth from the curious scrolls and
foliage surrounding them. In the middle of the cabinet was
carved the full-length figure of a man, who seemed to be
perpetually grinning, perhaps at himself, for in truth he was
a most ridiculous figure. He had crooked legs like a goat,
small horns on his forehead, and a long beard. The children
of the house used to call him 'Field-Marshal-Major-
General-Corporal-Sergeant Billy-goat's legs'. This was a
long, hard name, and not many figures, in wood or stone,
could boast of such a title. There he stood, his eyes always
fixed upon the table under the mirror; for on this table
stood a pretty little porcelain shepherdess, her mantle
gathered gracefully round her and fastened with a red rose.
Her shoes and hat were gilt, her hand held a crook; she
was a most charming figure. Close by her stood a little
chimney-sweep as black as coal, and made like the shepherdess of porcelain. He was as clean and neat as any other
china figure. Indeed, the manufacturer might just as well
have made a prince of him as a chimney-sweep, for though
elsewhere black as a coal, his face was as fresh and rosy as
a girl's, which was certainly a mistake—it ought to have
been black. With his ladder in his hand, he kept his place
close by the little shepherdess. They had been put side by
side from the first, had always remained on the same spot,
and so had plighted their troth to each other. They suited

each other for they were both young, both of the same kind of china, and both alike fragile and delicate.

Near them stood another figure three times as large as they were, and also made of porcelain. He was an old Chinese mandarin who could nod his head, and he declared that he was grandfather of the little shepherdess. He could not prove this, but he insisted that he had authority over her; and so, when 'Field-Marshal-Major-General-Corporal-Sergeant Billy-goat's legs' made proposals to the little shepherdess, he nodded his head in token of his consent.

'Now you will have a husband,' said the old mandarin to her, 'who, I verily believe, is made of mahogany. You will be the wife if a Field-Marshal-Major-General-Corporal-Sergeant, of a man who has a whole cabinet full of silver plate, besides a store of no one knows what in the secret drawers.'

'I will not go into that dismal cabinet,' said the little shepherdess. 'I have heard that he has eleven china wives already imprisoned there.'

'Then you shall be the twelfth, and you will be in good company,' said the Chinaman. 'This very night, as soon as you hear a noise in the old cabinet you shall be married, as sure as I am a mandarin;' and then he nodded his head and fell asleep.

But the little shepherdess wept, and turned to her betrothed, the china chimney-sweep.

'I believe I must beg you,' said she, 'to go out with me into the wide world, for we cannot stay here.'

'I will do everything you wish,' said the chimney-sweep; 'let us go at once. I think I can support you by my profession.'

'If we could but get safely off the table!' sighed she. 'I shall never be happy till we are really out in the world.'

Then he comforted her, and showed her how to set her little foot on the carved edges and gilded foliage twining round the leg of the table. He helped her with his little ladder, and at last they reached the floor. But when they turned to look at the old cabinet, they saw that it was all astir: the carved stags were putting their little heads farther out, raising their antlers and moving their throats, whilst 'Field - Marshal - Major - General - Corporal - Sergeant Billy-goat's legs' was jumping up and down and shouting to the old Chinese mandarin, 'Look, they are running away! they are running away!' The runaways were dreadfully frightened, and jumped into an open drawer under the window-sill.

In this drawer there were three or four packs of cards, none of them complete, and also a little puppet-theatre which had been set up, as neatly as it could be. A play was then going on, and all the queens, whether of diamonds, hearts, clubs, or spades, sat in the front row fanning themselves with the flowers they held in their hands, while behind them stood the knaves, showing that they had each two heads, one above and one below, as most cards have. The play was about two persons who were crossed in love, and the shepherdess wept over it, for it was just like her own story.

'I cannot bear this!' said she. 'Let us leave the drawer.' But when they again got to the floor, on looking up at the table, they saw that the old Chinese mandarin was awake, and that his whole body was shaking to and fro with rage.

'Oh, the old mandarin is coming!' cried the little shepherdess, and down she fell on one knee in the greatest distress.

'A thought has struck me,' said the chimney-sweep. 'Let us creep into the large pot-pourri vase that stands in the corner; there we can rest upon roses and lavender, and throw salt in his eyes if he come near us.'

'That will not do at all,' said she; 'for many years ago the mandarin was betrothed to the pot-pourri vase, and there is always a kindly feeling between people who have been so intimate as that. No there is no help for it; we must wander forth together into the wide world!'

'Have you indeed the courage to go with me into the wide world?' asked the chimney-sweep. Have you thought how large it is, and that we may never return?'

'I have,' replied she.

The chimney-sweep looked fixedly at her, and when he saw that she was firm, he said, 'My path leads through the chimney. Have you indeed the courage to creep with me through the stove, through the fire-box and up the pipe? I know the way well! We shall climb up so high that they cannot come near us, and at the top there is a hole that leads into the wide world.'

He led her to the door of the stove.

'How black it looks!' sighed she, but she went on with him, through the fire-box and up the pipe, where it was dark, pitch dark.

'Now we are in the chimney,' said he; 'and look, what a lovely star shines over us.'

And it really was a star, shining right down upon them, as if to show them the way. So they climbed and crawled; it was a fearful path, so dreadfully steep and seemingly endless, but the little sweep lifted her and held her, and showed her the best places to plant her tiny porcelain feet on, till at last they reached the edge of the chimney. There they sat down to rest for they were very tired.

The sky with all its stars was above them, and the town with all its roofs lay beneath them. They would see all round them far out into the wide world. The poor little shepherdess had never dreamt of anything like this; she leant her little head on the chimney-sweep's arm, and wept so bitterly that the gilding broke off from her waistband.

'This is too much!' she cried. 'The world is all too large! Oh that I were once more upon the little table under the mirror! I shall never be happy till I am there again. I have followed you into the wide world; surely if you love me you can follow me home again.'

The chimney-sweep talked sensibly to her, reminding her of the old mandarin and 'Field-Marshal-Major-General-Corporal-Sergeant Billy-goat's legs'. But she wept so bitterly, and kissed her little chimney-sweep so fondly, that at last he could not but yield to her request, foolish as it was.

So with great trouble they crawled down the chimney, crept through the pipe and through the fire-box and into the dark stove. They lurked for a little behind the door, listening, before they would venture to return into the room. Everything was quite still. They peeped out. Alas! on the floor lay the old mandarin. In trying to follow the runaways, he had jumped down from the table and had broken into three pieces. His head lay shaking in a corner. 'The Field - Marshal - Major - General - Corporal - Sergeant Billy-goat's legs' stood where he had always stood, thinking over what had happened.

'Oh, how shocking!' exclaimed the little shepherdess. 'My old grandfather is broken in pieces, and it is all our fault! I shall never get over it!' and she wrung her little hands.

'He can be put together again,' said the chimney-sweep. 'He can very easily be put together; only don't be so impatient! If they glue his back together, and put a strong rivet in his neck, then he will be as good as new, and will be able to say plenty of unpleasant things to us.'

'Do you really think so?' asked she. And then they climbed up the table to the place where they had stood before.

'Well, we're not much farther on,' said the chimney-sweep; 'we might have spared ourselves all the trouble.'

'If we could but have old grandfather put together!' said the shepherdess. 'Will it cost very much?'

He was put together. The family had his back glued and his neck riveted. He was as good as new, but could no longer nod his head.

'We have certainly grown very proud since we were broken in pieces,' said Field-Marshal-Major-General-Corporal-Sergeant Billy-goat's legs, 'but I must say, for my part, I do not see that there is anything to be proud of. Am I to have her or am I not? Just answer me that!'

The chimney-sweep and the little shepherdess looked

On the floor lay the old mandarin, broken into three pieces

imploringly at the old mandarin; they were so afraid lest he should nod. But nod he could not, and it was disagreeable to him to have to tell a stranger that he had a rivet in his neck. So the young porcelain people were left together, and they blessed the grandfather's rivet, and loved each other till they broke in pieces.

BIG CLAUS AND LITTLE CLAUS

Once upon a time there lived in the same village two men bearing the same name. One of them had four horses, the other had only one; so to distinguish them from each other, the owner of four horses was called 'Big Claus', and he who owned only one horse was known as 'Little Claus'.

All the week long Little Claus had to plough for Big Claus, and to lend him his one horse, and in return Big Claus lent him his four horses, but only for one day in the week, Sunday. Then Little Claus was a proud man, and smacked his whip over the five horses, all his for this one day at least. The people, dressed in their best, were walking to church, and as they passed they looked at Little Claus, ploughing with his five horses; and he was so pleased that he kept cracking his whip and crying our, 'Hurrah! five fine horses, and all mine!'

'You must not say that,' said Big Claus; 'for only one of the horses is yours.'

But Little Claus soon forgot, and when another party passed by, cried out again, 'Hurrah! five fine horses, all mine!'

'Did not I tell you not to say that?' cried Big Claus very angrily. 'If you say that again, I shall strike your one horse dead on the spot, and then there'll be an end to your boasting.'

'Oh, but I'll never say it again, indeed I won't,' said Little Claus, and he quite meant to keep his word. But presently more people came by, and when they nodded a friendly 'Good-morning' to him, he was so delighted, and it seemed to him such a grand thing to have five horses to plough his bit field, that he flourished his whip and cried out, 'Hurrah! five fine horses, every one of them mine!'

'I'll soon cure you of that!' cried Big Claus in a fury, and taking up a stone he flung it at the head of Little Claus's horse. So heavy was the stone that the poor creature fell down dead.

'Oh, now I have no horse at all!' cried Little Claus, weeping. But after a little he set to work to flay the dead horse, and he dried the skin thoroughly in the air. Then, putting the dried skin into a sack, he slung it across his shoulders, and set out to the nearest town to sell it. He had a long way to go, and had to pass through a large dark wood. Here a fierce storm burst forth, and the clouds, the rain, and the dark shaking firs, so bewildered poor Claus that he lost his way, and before he could find it night came down. Not far off stood a large farm-house. The shutters were closed, but Little Claus could see lights shining through the cracks at the top of the shutters. He went up to the house, and knocked at the door. The farmer's wife opened the door, but when she heard what he wanted she told him he must ask elsewhere. He couldn't come into her house; her husband was from home, and she couldn't let in a stranger in his absence.

'Well then, I must sleep outside,' said Little Claus, as the farmer's wife shut the door in his face.

Near the farm-house stood a hay-stack, and between it and the house was a little shed with a flat straw roof.

'I can sleep up there,' thought Little Claus when he saw the roof. 'It will make a capital bed, but I hope the stork may not take it into his head to fly down and bite my legs.' For a stork had made his nest on the roof, and had mounted guard beside the nest, as wide-awake as could be, although it was night.

So Little Claus crept up on the roof of the shed, and there he turned and twisted about till he had made himself comfortable. The shutters he found did not close properly at the top, so that he could see all that went on in the room below. There he saw a large table spread with bread and wine, roast meat and fried fish. The farmer's wife and the sexton were sitting at table. She was pouring out a glass of wine for him, and he was eagerly helping himself to a large slice of fish—he happened to be particularly fond of fish. 'It's really too bad of them to keep it all to themselves!' sighed Little Claus. 'Oh, how I should like some!' and he crept as near to the window as he could. What a fine cake he could see now! Why, this was quite a feast!

Just then he heard the tramp of hoofs coming down the road to the farm-house. It was the farmer riding home.

The farmer was a real good-hearted fellow, but he had one strange weakness, he could not bear to see a sexton; the sight of one made him half mad. Now, the sexton of the neighbouring town was first cousin to the farmer's wife, and they were old playmates and good friends; so, knowing that the farmer would be from home this evening, he came to pay his cousin a visit; and the good woman, being pleased to see him, had put before him the best she had in her larder. Now, when she heard the tramp of the farmer's horse, she was frightened and bade the sexton creep into a large empty chest that stood in a corner. He did so, for he knew that the farmer would be almost wild if he came in and found a sexton in the room. The woman then hastened to hide the wine, and put the dishes inside her baking-oven, for fear her husband, if he saw the table spread with them, should ask for whom she had been preparing such a grand feast.

'Oh dear, oh dear!' sighed Little Claus on the top of the shed, when he saw the good things put out of sight.

'Anybody up there?' asked the farmer on hearing the noise; and he looked up and saw Little Claus. 'Why are you lying up there?' Come down and come into the house with me.'

So Little Claus came down and told the farmer how he had lost his way, and begged him for lodgings for the night.

'To be sure,' said the good-natured man. 'Come in quickly, and let's have something to eat.'

The woman received them kindly, covered one end of the long table with a cloth and placed on it a large basin of porridge. The farmer was hungry and ate his porridge with a capital appetite, but Little Claus could not eat for thinking of the roast meat, the fish, the wine, and the nice cake that he had seen stowed away in the oven. He had put the sack containing the horse's skin under the table, and now, as he did not relish the porridge, he trod on the sack till the dry skin squeaked quite loud.

'Hush!' muttered Little Claus to his sack, at the same time treading on it again, so as to make it squeak even louder than before.

'What have you got in your sack?' asked the farmer.

'Oh! I've got a little conjurer there,' replied Little Claus, 'and he says we need not be eating porridge when he has conjured a feast of beef-steak, fried fish, and cake, into the oven on purpose for us.'

'A conjurer did you say?' cried the farmer, and starting up he looked into the oven, and there, to be sure, were fish, and steak, and cake. They had been hidden there by the farmer's wife, and the thought it was the work of the conjurer under the table. The farmer's wife durst not say a word. Almost as bewildered as her husband, she set the food on the table, and the farmer and his guest began with a hearty appetite to eat of the good cheer.

Presently Little Claus trod on his sack again, and again the skin squeaked.

'What does your conjurer say now?' asked the farmer.

'He says,' replied Little Claus, 'that there are three bottles of wine for us standing just in the corner of the oven.' So the woman was obliged to bring out the wine that she had hidden, and the farmer poured himself out a glass and enjoyed it. He thought it would be a fine thing to have such a capital conjurer as this.

'A proper conjurer this of yours!' said he at last. 'Do you think he could conjure up the Evil One? I should rather like to see him.'

'Of course,' answered Little Claus; 'my conjurer will do anything I ask him.—That you will, won't you?' said he, again treading on his sack—'Didn't you hear him say 'Yes'?' he asked. 'But I warn you he, the "Evil One", is

somewhat dark and unpleasant-looking, and you'll not like
to see him!'

'Oh, I shall not be afraid. What will he look like?'

'Why, he is for all the world just like a sexton.'

'A sexton!' said the farmer. 'That is a pity! You know
I cannot bear the sight of a sexton; but no matter, since
I shall know that it is not a real sexton, I shall not care
about it. Oh, I've plenty of courage, only don't let him
come too near me!'

'Well, I'll ask my conjurer again,' said Little Claus,
and he trod on his skin till it went 'squeak, squeak', and he
bent down to listen.

'What does he say now?' asked the farmer.

'He says you must open the large chest that stands in
the corner yonder. You have only to lift up the lid, and you
will see the Evil One crouching down inside; but you must
hold the lid firmly so that he cannot slip out.'

'Will you help me to hold the lid?' said the farmer;
and he went to the chest where his wife had hidden the real
sexton, who sat huddled up, trembling, and holding his
breath, lest he should be discovered.

The farmer raised the lid a little and peeped in. 'Ugh!'
cried he, springing back in affright, 'I saw him; he is
exactly like our sexton; oh, how horrible!'

Then he sat down at table again, and began to drink.
The wine revived his courage; and neither he nor his guest
ever thought of going to bed. There they sat, talking and
feasting, till late in the night.

'Do you know,' said the farmer at length, 'I should like
very much to have your conjurer; would you mind selling
him to me? Name your own price; I don't care if I give
you a whole bushel of money for it on the spot.'

'How can you ask such a thing?' said Little Claus
'He is such a useful and faithful servant. I would not
dream of parting with him for his weight in gold ten times
over.'

'I can't offer you so much gold,' said the farmer, 'but
all the same I should like very much to have him.'

'Really,' said Little Claus at length, 'since you have been so kind as to give me lodgings for the night, I do not think I can refuse your request. I will let you have my conjurer for a bushel of money—only the bushel must be crammed full, you know.'

'Certainly it shall,' answered the farmer; 'but you must take away the chest as well. I don't wish it to remain an hour longer in the house; it will always be reminding me of the hateful sexton-face I saw inside it.'

So the bargain was struck, and Little Claus gave the farmer his sack, with the dry skin in it, and got for it a bushel of money. The farmer also gave him a wheel-barrow to carry away the money and the chest.

'Farewell!' said Little Claus, as he wheeled away in the wheel-barrow the money and the chest with the sexton hidden in it.

On one side of the wood flowed a broad, deep river. The stream was so strong that no one could swim against it, so a bridge had lately been built over it. Little Clause took his way over the bridge, but stopped in the middle of it, saying loud enough to be heard by the sexton in the chest, 'Now, what on earth is the use of this great chest to me? It's as heavy as if it were filled with stones; and quite tires me out wheeling it along. I'll throw it out into the river: if it swims home after me, well and good; if not, it doesn't matter to me.'

Then he took hold of the chest and lifted it as if intending to throw it into the water.

'Don't do that, I beg of you,' cried the sexton from the inside of the chest; 'please let me out first.'

'Holloa!' cried Little Claus, pretending to be frightened; 'is the chest bewitched? If so, the sooner it's out of my hands the better.'

'Oh no, no, no,' cried the sexton; let me out, and I'll give you another whole bushel of money.'

'Ah, that's quite another matter,' said Little Claus; and he set down the chest, and lifted the lid; and out crept the sexton, greatly pleased at his escape. He kicked the

Out crept the sexton, greatly pleased at his escape

empty chest into the water, and then took Little Clause to his house with him, where he gave him the bushel of money he had promised. So Little Clause had now a wheel-barrow full of money.

'I have certainly been well paid for my horse's skin,' said he to himself, as he entered his own little room, and emptied his money in a heap on the floor. 'How vexed Big Clause will be when he finds how rich my horse's skin has made me. But I shall not tell him exactly how it all came about.' Then he sent a little boy to Big Claus to borrow a bushel-measure from him.

'What can he want with a bushel-measure, I wonder?' thought Big Claus, and he cunningly smeared the bottom of the measure with clay, hoping that some of whatever was measured might stick to it. And so it happened. And when the measure was brought back to him, he found three silver coins sticking to the bottom. 'Fine doings, upon my word!' cried Big Claus; and off he set to the house of his namesake, and demanded, 'Where did you get so much money?'

'For my horse's skins, which I sold yesterday,' was the answer.

'Are horses' skin so dear as that?' said Big Claus. 'Who would have thought it?' And he ran home, took an axe, knocked all his four horses on the head with it, and then flayed off the skins, and took them into the town to sell. 'Skins, skins, who will buy skins?' he cried as he went through the streets.

All the shoemakers and tanners in the town came running up to him, and asked what he wanted for them.

'A bushel of money for each,' replied Big Claus.

'Are you mad?' said they. 'Do you think we have money to spend by the bushel?'

'Skins, fresh skins, who will buy skins?' shouted he again; and still to all who asked how much he wanted for them he replied, 'A bushel of money.'

'The boor is trying to make fools of us,' said some one at last in great wrath. Then the shoemakers took their

straps and the tanners their leather aprons and they beat
Big Claus.

'Skins, fresh skins, fine fresh skins,' they mocked. 'And
let us mark his own skin till it is black and blue. Out of
the town with the great ass!' So they thrust Big Clause out
of the town.

'Little Clause shall pay for this,' muttered he. 'I'll beat
him to death.'

It so chanced that Little Claus's grandmother died that
evening. She had always been cross and ill-natured to him,
but he felt really sorry. So he lifted the dead woman and
laid her in his own warm bed, in hopes that the warmth
might bring her to life again. For his own part he thought
he could spend the night in a chair in a corner of the room
as he had often done before. About midnight the door
opened, and Big Clause came in with an axe in his hand.
He knew where Little Claus's bed stood, so he went straight
up to it, and struck the dead grandmother a violent blow
on the head, thinking it was Little Claus.

'There's for you,' cried he. 'Now you'll never make a
fool of me again.' And off he went home.

'What a wicked man he is,' sighed Little Claus. 'So he
wished to kill me. It was a good thing that grandmother
was dead already, or that blow would have hurt her very
much.'

Then he dressed his grandmother in her Sunday clothes,
borrowed a horse from a neighbour, yoked it to the cart,
set his grandmother on the back seat so that she might not
fall out when it was moving, and so drove away through
the wood. At sunrise they came to a large inn, and there
Little Claus pulled up and went in to get something to eat.
The landlord was a wealthy and a good man, but he was as
quick-tempered as if he had been made of pepper and snuff.

'Good-morning!' said he to Little Claus. 'You are early
astir today.'

'Yes!' said Little Claus. 'I am going to the town with
my grandmother; she is sitting at the back of the cart.
But I cannot bring her into the room; will you, yourself,

not take her a glass of mead? But you must speak very loud for she does not hear well.'

'I'll do that,' said the landlord, and he poured out a large glass of mead, and went out with it to the grand-mother who was sitting bolt upright in the cart.

'Hear is a glass of mead from your grandson,' said the landlord. But the dead woman did not answer a word, but sat quite still.

'Don't you hear?' bawled the landlord as loudly as he could. 'Here is a glass of mead from your grandson.' Again and yet again he yelled the same thing, and as she did not stir he lost his temper and threw the glass of mead in her face. It struck her on the nose, and she fell backwards into the cart, for she was only seated upright behind and not fastened.

'What! what!' cried Little Clause, rushing from the inn and seizing the landlord by the throat. 'You have killed my grandmother. See what a hole there is in her fore-head.'

'Oh, what a misfortune!' cried the landlord, wringing his hands. 'All this comes of my hasty temper. Dear Little Claus, I will bury your grandmother as if she were my own, and I will give you a bushel of money, if you will only say nothing about this. If it is known they will cut off my head, and that will be very unpleasant.'

So Little Clause got a bushel of money, and the landlord buried his grandmother as if she had been his own.

Then when Little Clause came home again with much money, he at once sent his boy again to Big Clause, asking him for the loan of a bushel-measure.

'What's this?' said Big Claus. 'Did I not kill him out-right? I must look into this myself.' So he himself went across with the bushel-measure to Little Claus. 'How did you come by all this money?' said he, his eyes almost starting out of his head, as he saw all the riches his neigh-bour had added.

'You murdered my grandmother instead of me,' said Little Clause. 'So I have sold her for a bushel of money.'

'That's a good price, at any rate,' said Big Claus. So he went home, took a hatchet and killed his own grandmother. Then he put her into a cart, drove to the town where an apothecary lived, and asked if he would buy a dead body.

'Who is it? and where did you get it?' asked the apothecary.

'It is my grandmother,' answered Big Claus. 'I have killed her, that I might get a bushel of money for her body.'

'God protect us!' said the apothecary. 'You are raving. If you say such things, you will have your head cut off.' And then he talked to him seriously about the wickedness of what he had done, and told him that such a crime should certainly not go unpunished. He frightened Big Clause so much that he rushed out of the Surgery, leapt into the cart, whipped up his horse, and drove home. The apothecary and all the people, thinking him mad, let him go where he would.

'You'll pay for this,' said Big Claus as soon as he got into the main road. 'Yes, you'll pay for this, Little Claus.' So, as soon as he got home, he took the largest sack he could find and went across to Little Clause and said: 'So, you have played me another trick. First I killed my horses, then my grandmother, and it is all your fault; but you shall no longer make a fool of me.' Then he caught Little Claus and bundled him bodily into the sack, which he threw over his shoulders, saying, 'Now, I am going to drown you.'

But he had a long way to walk before he reached the river, and Little Clause was no light weight to carry. The road led past the church. The organ was playing, for the service had just begun. Among the congregation Big Claus saw a man to whom he wished to speak. 'Little Claus cannot get out of the sack by himself,' thought he, 'and no one can help him, for all the people are in church. I shall just go in and call that man back into the porch for a minute.' So he set down the sack and ran into church.

'Oh dear, oh dear!' sighed Little Claus in the sack as he turned and twised in vain efforts to loosen the string with which the sack was tied. Just then a very old drover passed by. His hair was white as snow, and he had a stout staff in his hand with which he was driving a large herd of cows and bullocks before him, many more, indeed, than he, weak as he was, could manage. One of them knocked against the sack, and turned it over and over. 'Ah, yes!' cried Little Claus, 'I am still so young; and I am soon going to heaven,'

'And I, poor fellow,' said the old drover, 'am already so old; and yet I cannot get there.'

'Open the sack,' said Little Claus. 'Creep into it instead of me, and then in an instant you will be in heaven.'

'Yes, with right good will I shall do so,' said the old drover. And he opened the sack from which Little Claus sprang forth.

'Will you look after my cattle?' said the old drover as he crept into the sack; and Little Claus tied up the sack, and walked off with all the cows and bullocks.

Presently Big Claus came running back. He took up the sack, and flung it again across his shoulders. It seemed to have grown lighter, for the old drover was not half so heavy as Little Claus. 'How much lighter the burden seems now,' said he. 'It must be because I have been hearing a psalm.' So on he trudged to the river, which was deep and broad, and flung the sack with the old drover in it whom he thought to be Little Claus out into the water, and shouted after it, 'There now, Little Claus, you shall never cheat me more!' He then turned homewards, but on passing a place where two roads crossed, whom should he meet but Little Claus with his cattle.

'How comes this?' said Big Claus. 'Is it really you? Did not I drown you, then?'

'Yes,' said Little Claus. 'You threw me into the river half an hour ago.'

'But how did you come by all these beautiful cattle?' asked Big Claus.

'These are sea-cattle,' said Little Claus. 'I'll tell you the whole story. Thank you for drowning me; it has made me rich, really very rich. I was frightened when I lay in the sack, and the wind whistled in my ears when you threw me down from the bridge into the river. I sank to the bottom at once, but I was not hurt, for I fell on the softest, freshest grass. Immediately the sack opened, and the most beautiful little girl came towards me. She was dressed in white and wore a wreath of green leaves. She took me by the hand and said, "So you are come, Little Claus! Here are some cattle of yours; and a mile farther up the road another and larger herd is grazing; I will give you that herd also." Then I saw that the river was a sort of highway for the people of the sea, and that on it they walked and drove to and fro from the sea far up into the land where the river rises, and thence back to the sea again. No place can be more beautiful than the bottom of the river is. It is covered with the prettiest flowers and the sweetest, freshest grass. The fish swam past me as swiftly as the birds fly in the air; and what gaily-dressed people I saw there, and what fine cattle grazed on the hills and in the valleys!'

'Then why were you in such a hurry to come up again?' asked Big Claus; 'if it was all so beautiful down there I don't think I'd have come back.'

'Did not I tell you,' said Little Claus, 'that the sea-lady told me that a mile up the road—and by the road she could only mean the river, she can't come into our land roads—there was another and larger herd of cattle for me? But I knew that the river makes a great many turns, and I thought I'd save myself half a mile by taking the short cut across the land. So here I am, you see, and I shall soon get to my sea-cattle!'

'What a lucky fellow you are!' exclaimed Big Claus. 'Don't you think that I might have some cattle too, if I went down to the bottom of the river?'

'How can I tell?' asked Little Claus.

'You envious scoundrel! You want to keep all the beautiful sea-cattle for yourself, I warrant!' cried Big Claus. 'Either you will carry me to the water's edge, and throw me over, or I will kill you! Make your choice!'

'Oh, please don't be angry!' entreated Little Claus. 'I cannot carry you in the sack to the river, you are too heavy for me; but if you will walk there yourself, and then creep into the sack, I will throw you over with all the pleasure in the world!'

'But if I find no sea-cattle, I shall kill you all the same when I come back, remember that!' said Big Claus.

They walked together to the river. As soon as the cattle saw the water, they ran on as fast as they could, eagerly crowding against each other, and all wanting to drink first.

'Only look at my sea-cattle!' said Little Claus. 'See how they are longing to be at the bottom of the river.'

'That's all very well,' said Big Claus, 'but you must help me first.' And he quickly crept into a great sack which had lain stretched across the shoulders of one of the oxen. 'Put a heavy stone in with me,' said he, 'else, perhaps, I shall not sink to the bottom.'

'No fear of that!' replied Little Claus. However, he put a large stone into the sack, tied the strings, and pushed the sack into the water. Plump! there it fell straight to the bottom.

'I am much afraid he will not find his sea-cattle!' observed Little Claus, and he drove his own herd home to the village.

OTHER TITLES IN THIS SERIES